DEAD EVIDENCE

The Complete

Cases of Harrigan

ED LYBECK

---

introduction by Will Murray

illustrations by Arthur Rodman Bowker

cover by Jes Schlaikjer

BLACK MASK

2020

Associate Editor: Ray Riethmeier
The publisher would like to acknowledge John L. Locke for his assistance in compiling this collection.

Table of Contents

Introduction

EDWARD LYBECK MAY be one of the most obscure contributors to *Black Mask* magazine during the early 1930s. His career was painfully short-lived. Fewer than thirty pulp stories were published over a five-year period.

So it's surprising to read in an old writer's magazine that he was considered one of the rising stars of 1932.

Here is what editor-writer Wallace R. Bamber wrote in his 1932 *Author & Journalist* essay, "Let's Face the Facts, Pulp Writers!" This was a time when the Great Depression was hammering the pulp industry and those who wrote for it. Bamber believed that the pulp story must change radically in order to survive, and that if it did, a new golden age of fiction would dawn.

> The time is here now for another abrupt change. Every sign predicates it. As to what the pulp story of the future will be I don't profess to know. […] My hint, to those who don't even care to guess just what the future pulp story will be, is to read the present-day stories of Dashiell Hammett, George Bruce, Theodore Roscoe, Chester L. Saxby, Ed Lybeck and Doane R. Hoag. And now I suppose you are exclaiming: "Who is Lybeck? Who is Hoag?" Taking it for granted, of course, that you recognize the first four names; which you will if you are at all familiar with pulps. Ed Lybeck and Doane R. Hoag are young writers who have caught this new trend, and may turn out to be the H. Bedford-Jones's and J. Allan Dunns of the future golden age. You are welcome to keep

this copy of THE AUTHOR & JOURNALIST for twenty years, and check up on me later. It is my idea that the above mentioned writers have something now of what the pulp story of the future will be.

This is heady praise for a writer who had been in the business for half a year. But as a prediction, it was wildly off the mark. Neither Ed Lybeck or the equally obscure Doan R. Hoag were writing fiction in 1942, much less 1952.

Ever the canny editor, Joseph T. Shaw did not make a big noise about Ed Lybeck when he rolled out his first two stories. Shaw thought he would leave it to the readers to praise or knock the new writer.

As he wrote in the February 1932 issue, "So—when Ed Lybeck came along with 'Leaded Ink,' (in December) and 'Kick-Back' (in January) we merely printed the stories and sat back."

Initial reaction was strong and positive. One reader said: "Regarding Ed Lybeck's 'Leaded Ink,' it's a sizzler. Hold Lybeck. You've got something. His opening paragraph was worth the $.20."

Then, quoting from "a magazine editor who is also a writer himself," came this:

It isn't often that I drag the mill up in front of me and write fan letters to editors of magazines. Reason being perhaps that I am in the game and I have a faint inkling of what it is all about. But I do appreciate merit in anything, and I think you have it in the current issue of *Black Mask*.... I read all the stories and the current issue and didn't find a single dud. What's more, "Leaded Ink" by

Ed Lybeck was one of the fastest-moving yarns I've ever read in my life, and by far the best-written yarn in the book. I don't know this boy from a bar of soap, but I do know the others, but, despite that, I hand the palm to the newcomer. If he can keep up to that pace, he will be a whirlwind.... Lybeck has a rip-roaring style that carries along with the speed of lightning with an extra kick in the pants every so often to further bewilder you and take your breath away, and even if I he doesn't succeed in crowding quite as much story in his next yarn, I feel that it will be plenty good for *Black Mask*—or any other book....

Inasmuch as Wallace Bamber was one of the few editor-writers in the game at that time, it's not too much of a stretch to assert that Bamber was this anonymous booster!

Ed Lybeck wrote only four stories for *Black Mask,* all starring Francis St. Xavier Harrigan, a former gunman who switched to reporting for the New York *Leader.* Harrigan probably did as much gunslinging as reporting—and maybe more—when contrasted with his earlier outlaw exploits.

In that sense, Harrigan was a little like author Lybeck himself, if we can believe the staccato biography Joe Shaw ran in the March 1932 issue of *Black Mask* magazine. A tough guy who danced on the wrong side of the law before going straight.

ED LYBECK—born in North Shields, England, in 1905. In Sweden seven years. Been all over Europe, this country and Canada. Experience—high, wide and handsome; hoboed it; railroad maintenance-man; circus roustabout; semi-pro ball-player; mill-worker; typewriter inspector; claim-auditor for an insurance company, and sundry other things thrown in for fair measure. Took a peek on the inside of the ale-and-alky racket; rode out a shotgun barrage on the Mohawk Trail one night and got the bright idea there might be safer ways of getting the buck. He used to be six feet, but after that night's experience decided five feet ten one-half would collect a lot less buckshot—so he settled down and started to whang the old typewriter. Sometimes thinks—like Joe Cardinale—it's the old machine-gun he's playing. (Now we know how Harrigan gets his kick and who put the "lead" in "Leaded Ink.")

Add office boy, waiter, carpenter, and professional dancer to that long list. And although he never admitted to it in the print during his fictioneering days, Ed Lybeck had worked as a Democratic political operative, helping elect Al Smith Governor of New York in 1926. He was working as a lowly elevator operator in Manhattan's Willard Parker Hospital when he broke into *Black Mask*.

Of course, pulpster biographies were often exaggerated, if not downright fictitious. But Lybeck's probably hewed close to reality since this was *Black Mask* magazine, whose contributors were expected to know what they were writing about.

The first example of Ed Lybeck's work I have found was a dramatized true tale syndicated to newspapers in November 1931. "'Gator Justice" concerned an exploit of Federal narcotic agent Damon Vance. An accompanying biographical note claimed that Lybeck had previously contributed to periodicals, magazines and newspapers, and preferred to write true stories. But this and Lybeck's simultaneous debut in *Black Mask* are the earliest discoverable appearances of his name.

Francis St. Xavier Harrigan debuted in the December 1931 issue with "Leaded Ink." Two more gunsmokey exploits followed in quick succession. All three recounted the reporter's running battles with crooked "Reform" politician Frank Crocker and his bloodthirsty "chief of strafe," Icy Yeager. After that, Lybeck appeared to switch allegiance to *The Underworld Magazine* and became prolific for that Carwood title, producing fourteen stories over the next two years.

Why did he drop out of *Black Mask?* We can only surmise. Carwood was a slow payer, and did not offer top rates. More importantly, Joe Shaw was a tough editor. Like his contemporary at *Weird Tales*, Farnsworth Wright, Cap Shaw often made his writers revise and revise their manuscripts before finding them printworthy. *Black Mask* had a reputation as the toughest pulp magazine to crack. It was richly deserved. Competition to make its contents page was fierce. And Shaw had his regulars, whom readers demanded to see as often as possible.

The title's 128 pages per month could not be stretched to include extra stories. No doubt many good stories were turned down in favor of greater ones. Perhaps it was simply that editor Tom Wood of *The Underworld* was less demanding than was Shaw.

When his string ran out at Carwood, Lybeck managed to place a final Harrigan story with *Black Mask* in 1934, after which his novelettes appeared largely in the Thrilling magazine chain, with stray short stories in *Complete Underworld Novelettes, Clues* and *The Shadow Magazine*. Lybeck had a couple of minor series characters running at that time, but they each appeared only twice.

The last known Ed Lybeck pulp story appeared in *Thrilling Detective*, July 1936. Then he moved on. But to where? And what? Did he career continue under another name? Perhaps.

But by 1936, he was no longer a rising star, but a falling one, toiling for Thrilling and replaced by more industrious pulpsters such as Theodore Tinsley and Raymond Chandler in the pages of *Black Mask*. Would it be funny if he switched to writing under Thrilling house names like C.K.M. Scanlon? I doubt if he would have stooped to ghosting the Phantom Detective, but I can almost see Lybeck writing a Dan Fowler *G-Man* novel.

Although sources give his full name as Edward Arvid Lybeck, that was in fact not his birth name. He was born Charles Edward Widegren in 1905. After his mother remarried, he took the last name of his mother's second husband, Arvid Anders Lyback, having it legally changed in 1912. That was the year his father—Carl Charles Peter Widegren—perished in the sinking of the *Titanic*.

Lybeck lived for years in Wakefield, Massachusetts, moved to Connecticut and then Manhattan, eventually relocating to Los Angeles in 1935. He was still listed in the census as a fiction writer as late as 1940. During World War II, he owned a sheet metal shop, which closed due to the wartime scarcity of material. His career after that is unclear, but he soon moved into Los Angeles government, holding several administrative positions, then restarting his old career as a political operative, along with his wife, working for Congressman Thomas F. Ford of Pasadena. For a time, he was an employee of the Los Angeles Department of Water and Power, which prevented him from undertaking political work, but his wife remained active in public affairs.

Beginning in 1944, Lybeck served as an aide to Broadway actress-turned-politician Helen Gahagan Douglas, whom Richard Nixon defeated during the 1950 California senate race after smearing her as a Communist sympathizer, notoriously branding her the "pink lady." His wife, Ruth, was her secretary. Lybeck ghostwrote several of Douglas' speeches, and grew to become an excellent campaign manager because he knew the people and district of Los Angeles very well.

After that, Lybeck served as special assistant to Howard L. Holtzendorff, former Director of the City Housing Authority, and was questioned before a 1953 hearing pertaining to illegal contributions made by City Housing Authority to political campaigns furthering public housing.

When questioned if he knew that it was illegal to participate in Proposition 10, Lybeck replied in the breezy manner of a *Black Mask* hero, "I told them I didn't know it. And, that if it was illegal, I was sure guilty."

By the 1954, Lybeck was back in politics—if he ever left it—serving as campaign manager to Democratic Representative James Roosevelt. He had the title of field representative when he passed away a decade later.

Edward Lybeck died in June 1965, at the age of 60, a year to the month after his wife, who had worked as Roosevelt's executive assistant.

When Joseph T. Shaw began assembling his famous *The Hard-boiled Omnibus* for Simon and Schuster a decade after he left *Black Mask*, Frederick L. Nebel was one of a handful of former contributors who refused to let one of his vintage stories come back into print, so Shaw cast around for a suitable substitute.

Writing to his editor, Shaw offered Lybeck's "Kick-Back," saying, "… see if, in your opinion, it is too tough for us."

Apparently there was a concern that the stories appearing

in *The Hard-boiled Omnibus* not be absolutely hard-boiled, but semi-hard boiled. No matter.

Editor Lee Wright wrote back: "You're right that Ed Lybeck's story, KICKBACK, is very tough indeed. However, it seems to me a good example of the school at its most intense, and I think we might very well include it."

And that was how Ed Lybeck came back into print ten years after he drifted away from the fiction field.

Except for "Kick-Back," none of the other Harrigan stories have seen the light of day since the early 1930s. We're proud to bring them all back into print at long last.

Ed Lybeck was a rising *Black Mask* star in the days of Dashiell Hammett and Raymond Chandler. Does his work still hold up? Is his reputation as a cutting-edge crime writer still valid? Or is he a deservedly forgotten footnote in the Hard-boiled School of mystery writing? Read his Harrigan stories, and decide for yourself.

Leaded Ink

A Tommie handler bucks a man who slings ink

CARDINALE HAD ATTAINED perfection. His equal had yet to be found. When he played his typewriter he hit about seventeen keys a second; when he took dictation he never asked for a repeat; he'd never made a mistake and he loved his work.

You'd like a stenographer like Cardinale, eh? The hell you would!

Cardinale's typewriter was a stuttering, clacking, Thompson-gun; the dictation he took was the name and address of any person you'd pay two thousand dollars to get rid of and he hadn't made any mistakes because the first time he made one, he wouldn't have been around any more.

Joe Cardinale was dark, slim, medium-tall and an ice-cold killer. With a gun in his hand, he feared neither man nor devil. If someone had flagged your number and slipped Cardinale the necessary two grand, you were plenty through! It didn't make any difference who you were.

Maybe Joe was a little nutty in his way of regarding human life. It just didn't mean anything to him. He followed the star of his vanity and if a man stood in his way, let that man beware. Alienists would have called him a psychopathic. You and I would have called him a murderer.

There is little profit in trying to explain the Cardinales and Crowleys and Burkes. Nobody agrees about them; least of all, the experts. One says: "Environment"; another says: "Society"; a third says: "Heredity." But mostly—take it or leave it—it's an unhallowed union of Vanity and Laziness.

Joe Cardinale, born in the street and raised in a reform school, had all the predatory instincts of a savage alley cat. He knew he wasn't as good as the best and the knowledge galled him. But he had an out. It's an old saying that King Colt made all men equal. Joe bought a gun and began to chin himself on his egotism.

He squawked that the world was tight; that you couldn't get anything except at the point of a gun. He found out different. The State of New York, absolutely unasked, gave him a ticket to Great Meadow and a two-year board-bill all paid up.

That did it.

Great Meadow was full of punks. Full of cheap yeggs and cheaper con-men. They were all afraid of their shadows and they clustered to Cardinale. He was a natural. His coldness, his boastful hardness, his braggart vanity, made him a leader.

He knifed a guard in the back with a soup-spoon stiletto. The wound wasn't serious and they couldn't prove he'd done it, so they shellacked him and let it go. He gained local renown. He was the convict boss. The yellow punks worshiped him. Within Great Meadow's limits, he was famous.

When his time was up, he drifted back to the Big Town. Nobody knew him; nobody gave a damn. He was just a heel among heels. A private in the ranks. And Joe didn't like it.

Within Great Meadow's walls, he had tasted the heady wine of leadership. It buzzed in his brain; it twitched at his body; it tore at the roots of his colossal vanity. He bought another gun and burned off hundreds of rounds in the wooded shadows of the Palisades. He brooded on crashing the gate to Fame. He considered murdering some prominent person to show that he meant business. He'd almost settled on Aaron Klein,

Blue Ribbon of New York's shyster lawyers, when Prohibition descended on the land.

The graft was enormous. There were places for all. The effect on Joe was inevitable. He became in quick succession, protection-man, hi-jacker and bodyguard. Money poured in on him in agreeable quantities; there were occasional bits of hot action; life was easy—yet something lacked. Joe was a "good man,"—"reliable in a brush," but that was all. It wasn't enough.

Joe's vanity burned with a consuming flame. Torpedoes were a dime a dozen. To rule New York as he'd ruled Great Meadow—that would be something!

Opportunity comes to us all. It came to Joe Cardinale. He heard that Monte Ruffo, the beer king, was wanted out of the way. The job would be well paid. There would be fall-money and a mouthpiece if anything went wrong. The way would be greased for the killer. But killings weren't so common in those early days and nobody wanted the job. Hired guns laid off. They were leery of big killings; they still remembered Rosenthal.

Joe saw his chance. He muscled boldly in on a conference of Red Frank DeNegro and his lieutenants.

He began with no preliminaries whatsoever. "I hear you could get along without Ruffo," he said.

"Where'd'ya hear that?" snapped the thin-lipped DeNegro. "An' who da hell're you, anyway?"

"Never mind—to both questions!" This was no stripling private in the anti-social ranks. Neither was it a seventy-five-dollar-a-ride protection guy. This was the man who had blasted away with an automatic until it had become almost a part of him. The man who had coolly considered the rubbing-out of Aaron Klein as an introduction of himself to Gangland. The man who was probably New York City's foremost authority on the psychopathic ego.

This was the man whose narrow-lidded black eyes blazed into DeNegro's astonished face and whose hoarse, low voice rasped: "Never mind—to both questions! I heard you wanted a job done, that's all. I'll do it. My price is two grand; half on the line an' half to General Delivery after the job."

"Don't want much, do ya, feller?" sneered Tony Martello, one of DeNegro's lieutenants.

"Shut up!" said Cardinale coldly; "I'm talkin' to your boss. My price is tops, DeNegro, but there'll be no war chest. I don't want fall money or mouthpieces. If I stumble, I take my own raps."

DeNegro's heavy-lidded eyes flickered. He said: "You mean if you take a fall you'll ride de lightnin' widout a squawk?"

"I'll never ride the lightnin'," said Cardinale. "It's only dopes that want to live forever that keep the hot seat dusted. Me—I wouldn't even do another turn in stir."

Ruffo must go. DeNegro was desperate for a killer. As a last resort, he plunged on Cardinale. At least, he thought, the guy'd never live to collect the other grand.

He was wrong. The job was done with neatness and despatch and the balance duly collected. And three weeks later, Plug Reardon crossed Cardinale's palm with a thousand dollar bill and the boys bought flowers for Red Frank DeNegro.

But Plug Reardon made a mistake. He welched on the second installment. He held out the other thousand, and when Cardinale came for it, he laughed at Joe and told him to go to hell.

Cardinale measured him with narrowed eyes. He said: "You know how it goes with welchers, Reardon. With welchers and double-crossers."

Reardon sneered. "Yeah," he said, "an' that gives me an idea. Anybody's liable ta cross yuh." He looked meaningly at Butch Malloy, the gorilla who was his bodyguard. He said: "It ain't policy ta have a guy around that knows too much about these late killin's."

"Just what I was thinkin'!" said Cardinale, and dropped Reardon and Malloy with two shots that rang as one.

On the wall was a colored advertisement for Frontenac Ale. Cardinale ripped it down, wrote across the back of it: "To Services Rendered—$1,000.00" and under it he scrawled boldly, *"PAID IN FULL!"* He stuck it in Reardon's stiffening hand.

The police were hopelessly puzzled. That laconic, nonchalant receipt had them guessing. Then Park Row got it; there were newspapers in Park Row then. Some budding rewrite star called him the *"C.O.D. KILLER"* Cardinale's star was in the ascendant. In the joints and dives and hide-aways, "C.O.D." Cardinale was more famous than he had ever been within Great Meadow's walls.

He began to assemble a staff of his own. He gathered the trusted lieutenants and the prize torpedoes of the Big Shots he'd unloaded. Legal advice of the very best he got from Aaron Klein.

Klein was nobody's sap. He saw the new star on the gangster horizon and determined to benefit by its light. Politically powerful and backed by gangland connections, he had almost muscled himself into the District Attorneyship. But Harrigan of the *Leader* had made things too hot for him and Klein had bowed to Roger Coniston Muir. But Muir, an honest man and firm, was sick. Cancer, they said. So Klein grabbed off a special prosecutorship and settled down to confirm his power. It was an obscure job, but it rated an office at Criminal Courts and from there, Klein spread his devious net.

He was almost in control. Backed by a ruthless killer, he'd be hard to dislodge. Once Muir died, the town would see what it would see! Just let Cardinale get a rep—

Cardinale was getting it. He was feared everywhere. He collected tribute where and how he pleased. None dared say him nay. He killed gang-leaders indiscriminately until—suddenly—he was alone in the field. He was the uncrowned Czar of New York County's rackets. He was a one-man Unione Siciliane.

Then John Arthur Harms, lieutenant of detectives and prince of grafters, began to walk with heavy heels and—it was on Washington's Birthday—Cardinale bumped him off.

HARRIGAN WAS AT his desk when the news came in. More properly, he was *on* his desk. He was stretched full-length on it with his hat pulled over his eyes. He was saying, "For ——— sake, don't make so much noise! I haven't slept in two days."

Just whom he was talking to is hard to say. Reporters were shouting to each other, copy-boys were bustling about, rewrite men were clacking away at typewriters. In his private office, The Old Man was roaring at or to somebody. Downstairs the huge presses rumbled and clanked. Everywhere was clamor, confusion and noise. And on his desk, Harrigan pulled his hat over his eyes, said: "Shut up, everybody," and went to sleep.

Old Roger Conwell owned the *Leader* and his newspaper was a reflection of himself. He printed the news and to hell with the advertisers and he had a formula for firing a man. He would say: "What's your name?" You'd say: "Kelly, sir." He'd say: "Well, Kelly—good-bye." And you were through.

Old Roger had never set eyes on Harrigan before. He walked up to him and shook him gently by the arm.

Harrigan opened one eye. He said: "I don't know what you're selling but I don't want any." He closed the eye again.

Old Roger smiled wintrily. He said: "What's your name?"

The sleeper stirred slightly. "They call me Harrigan when I'm within earshot," he said.

"Well, Harrigan—" Old Roger Conwell rubbed his long nose. He remembered the lashings in print that had forced

Aaron Klein to abandon his plans to become District Attorney of New York County. He remembered the spectacular proofs of collusion between cops, crooks and prosecutors that had brought Lieutenant Harms up on charges. He remembered the veiled hints, the libelous half-proofs and, finally, the open charges that Joe Cardinale was the "C.O.D. Killer." All these stories and many others had blossomed on the front page of the *Leader* "By F. St. X. Harrigan, *Leader* Staff Correspondent."

Old Roger rubbed his long nose. He said: "Well, Harrigan—why the devil don't you go home and sleep?"

"Who ever heard of a newspaper man with a home?" grunted Harrigan. "Go away, please." And he slept on until the news of the Harms killing broke.

Young Billy Sullivan, fresh from college and enthusiastic about the Power of the Press, rushed up to him and shook him awake.

Sullivan was a sort of understudy to the *Leader's* erratic star. He was a kid from a cow-town college and he idolized Harrigan. When he came to New York he was young and dumb and an early riser. He thought the Eighteenth Amendment was a real Law and he wouldn't have known a verbal thunderbolt if he'd seen one on a push-cart. But Harrigan took a fancy to the kid and it wasn't long before Billy had a yen for Golden Wedding and a knack for pointed sarcasms.

"The Old Man wants you!" Sullivan was excited.

"The Old Man knows where he can find me," grumbled Harrigan sleepily.

"But it's a story! Lieutenant Harms has been murdered!"

"Then a lot of people are out of Harm's way," said Harrigan

and rolled over. Sullivan just caught the typewriter as it toppled floorward.

In the office, the City Editor was saying: "I'm sending Harrigan out right away."

"What's the use of antagonizing the whole police force, right off the bat?" growled the M.E. "Send Sullivan to pick up the surface. If there's something in the kindling, we'll unleash Harrigan to sniff it out. No hurry; the other rags wouldn't print it, anyway."

"But this might be some of the C.O.D. Killer's stuff," objected the City Editor. "Sullivan's young and he isn't in the know the way Harrigan is. He might stick his snoot into something and get it blown off!"

"Oh, hell!" said the M.E. "Don't be an ass! They won't kill a reporter. If they would, Harrigan wouldn't've lived a month. They don't dare. The Power of the Press—" But the City Editor was gone in quest of Sullivan.

HARRIGAN LEFT THE office five minutes after Billy Sullivan. He was in no hurry; it wasn't his story anyway and he wasn't greatly interested in the murder of John Arthur Harms. He'd seen it coming—had even written that one day machine-gun bullets would dig John Arthur's grave—but, after all, it was a killing. And he could help the kid out on his first big story; so he went.

Lieutenant Harms had gone to his death in a speakeasy. "Considerate of him," said Harrigan and had a whiskey sour.

The Gentlemen of the Press were just getting there. Cops and detectives were blowing in. The Coroner's physician had been sent for. John Arthur was lying huddled on the floor—

what was left of him. But nowhere, in the crowded back room of the speakie that had been turned into a death-chamber, was there any sign of Billy Sullivan.

Harrigan growled under his breath. Billy had fallen down. He'd have to write the story after all. He looked over the crowd again; in vain. He muttered: "The kid musta thought they wanted somethin' for the Sunday Supplement!"

There was a cop on guard at the door of the back room. Reporters were firing questions at him. He shrugged, said: "Don't know nuthin' about it. Just heard the shots an' came in. Here he was. Wasn't nobody with him." They turned towards the bullet-riddled wreck on the floor.

Harrigan walked over to the cop. He said: "Didn't see anythin' of a cub from the *Leader*, didya? Young guy—brown suit—gray hat—fulla questions?"

The cop scowled blackly. "I'll say I seen 'im," he growled; "I kicked 'im ta hell outta here!"

Harrigan was interested. "Yeah?" he said. "What'd he do?"

The cop nodded towards the murder room. "Prowled around in there when my back was turned. I catch 'im prowlin' around an' bendin' over the body an' he gets wise. I ask him how tha hell is the dicks gonna find out anythin' after he stumbles all over tha place an' he says: 'Tell 'em ta read tha papers.' I kicked 'im out!"

"An' he beat it, eh?"

The cop nodded. "Betcha life he did!"

Harrigan walked to the door, a crooked grin on his face. Sullivan was all right. He'd made no mistake in the kid. He'd beaten the cops to something, fed 'em with sarcasm and gone back to the office. He'd do.

No use spoiling the kid's story. If he'd found something, his was the credit. Harrigan walked out on the street. He'd have his fun from a different angle. No sport like throwing a knife at that louse of a Klein. The racketeering politician and Harms had always been thick as the thieves they were. Klein might still be at his office. He'd call him and ask for a comment on the sudden passing of a friend!

His lips quirked in a grin as he headed for a drug-store.

He dropped a nickel in the slot, jiggled the hook and asked for a number that wasn't in the Directory. The number of Aaron Klein's private wire was just one of the things that Harrigan wasn't supposed to know—and did.

There was some delay. It seemed Klein wasn't at his office. Harrigan muttered: "Damn it! Washington's Birthday!" He was impatient with himself and would have hung up except for a weakness common to us all. He wanted his nickel back.

Then—suddenly—a receiver was lifted and the voice of Aaron Klein said: "Hello; what is it?"

Harrigan's lips curled as he heard that well-known voice. He visualized the fat cheeks, the thick, oily nose with the pince-nez, the thick-lipped, pursed mouth of the shyster lawyer.

He said: "Hello, Klein. So you're answering telephones now, eh? When'd you get promoted?"

The gag died on his lips. There came to him plainly the sounds of a scuffle. A voice cried: "Help!" A voice that was close to the transmitter at the other end of the wire. It cried again: "Help! I'm—" Then a gun roared in Harrigan's ear. Roared twice, and with something that sounded like a mumbled: "My ———!" the receiver clicked.

Harrigan left the booth like a fireman going to a blaze at his sweetie's house. His heart pounded in his chest. That voice—the voice that cried: "Help!"—had been the voice of Billy Sullivan.

"My ———!" breathed Harrigan. "My ———! What've they done now!"

HUMAN EXPRESSION IS strangely circumscribed. Certain words—certain combinations of words—fit certain situations. When an unexpected situation arises, we unconsciously use the phrase that fits it, no matter how time-worn that phrase may be.

Harrigan, rushing out of a drug-store on Brewton Street, said: "My ———! What've they done now!"

Aaron Klein, political power and gangster lawyer, looking with horror-widened eyes at the lean, darkly sinister man with the smoking gun in his hand, said: "My ———! Cardinale! My ———! What've you done now!"

Cardinale bent and whipped a fountain pen from Billy Sullivan's vest pocket. The pen was green-and-black and on the fat barrel was stamped in gold letters the name of Aaron Klein. He tossed the pen on the desk and his black eyes glittered coldly. He said: "What'd you want me to do? He had us cold. It was you or him."

Klein's panic-frozen brain began to thaw. His flabby pasty cheeks became even flabbier as his mouth hung open. He said: "Me? Me!"

"Sure," said Cardinale. He said it as matter-of-factly as you'd mention the time of day. He walked through the empty outer office and locked the door. He came back. He said: "Sure, you. That pen was found where I musta dropped it—by Harms' body. It's got all kinds o' prints on it. They'd a wanted to know how it got there—what my prints were doing on it—how come I had your little toy. You couldn't a stood the gaff. You'd a cracked little by little an' I'd a hadda bump you." His tone was as casual as a man reading the weather report.

The shyster cringed as from a physical blow. For the first time, it was really brought home to him what manner of man this was. He had always considered himself superior to Cardinale. Superior in education, in position and in the office he held. Now, with those nonchalant words—"I'd a hadda bump you"— ringing in his ears, he realized fully that he was but a cog in Cardinale's machine, but a pawn in Cardinale's game, but a puppet who danced or died at Cardinale's whim. He covered his bloated, puffy face with shaking hands.

"Snap out of it," said Cardinale. "It's a holiday an' it's late an' there's nobody around but there will be soon an' you gotta meet 'em."

"Meet 'em?" said Klein dully. "Meet 'em? How am I going to explain this?" With averted face, he indicated the twisted, still form of Billy Sullivan.

"Leave it to me," said Cardinale. He drew a fat wallet from his pocket and extracted a bill. A smooth, unwrinkled, brand-new bill. The sort you dream about…. "This certifies that there has been deposited…. One Thousand Dollars… payable to the bearer on demand." He folded it twice, up and down, and stuck it in Sullivan's pocket. His upper vest-pocket. Just where it would be carried by a man to whom a thousand-dollar-bill was just one of those things, but who didn't want it seen in his wallet.

Klein looked on wide-eyed. He didn't get this at all.

Cardinale glanced up at him. "You're terrible dumb, Klein," he said pityingly. "I'm givin' you an out an' you can't even see it. That's a brand-new bill and the bank'll probably have the number of it an' know that it was issued to me. Even if they don't, it's too much money for a kid reporter to have. He's in the racket, d'ya see, an' there'll be very little squawk from the public once they know that. Just another chiseler blotted, see."

"But—"

"Shut up," said Cardinale curtly. "There isn't much time. People may be comin' up through the buildin' pretty soon, lookin' for those shots. I left MacFarlane an' Tony Martello in the car around the block. They'll be gettin' uneasy if I don't get back. An' cops'll be here soon, too. You gotta go on record. Grab that phone an' say: 'Police Headquarters! Emergency!' Say it as if you meant it, see. An' then say there's been a guy murdered in your office an' hang up. Snappy now; you're supposed to be excited."

Klein picked up the telephone. It shook in his hands. He said: "Police Headquarters! Quick!" His voice was squeaky and breaking. Cardinale's thin lips quirked. Klein didn't have to act. He sounded as if he'd just been through an earthquake.

The wires hummed. Cardinale silently opened a window. Klein's voice rose again, "Yes. Yes. This is Attorney Klein. I'm at my office—" His voice squeaked and broke. He began again: "I'm at my office in Criminal Courts. Come quick! There's been a man mur—" he stumbled over the word—"mur—killed in my office! My ———! Yes, he—"

Cardinale leaped forward and slammed down the hook, severing the connection.

"Put up that receiver, you punk!" he growled. "There you are, givin' 'em an argument an' you don't even know what you're supposed to say yet!"

On top of a dusty file-case in the corner of the room was an electric fan. Cardinale turned it towards the open window and plugged the connection. A miniature whirlwind swept through the room.

Klein hunched his ham-like shoulders around his fat-enfolded neck. "I'll get pneumonia," he protested querously.

"I hope so," said Cardinale. "It'll save me trouble."

"But what do you want that draft for?"

Cardinale wheeled on him. "I s'pose you want the whole Police Department walkin' in here an' the place reekin' o' cordite," he snapped. "The shots that killed this baby are supposed to've come from across the street. Don't forget that, you punk!"

"From—from across the street?"

"Sure. There're plenty o' offices over there an' they're all dark. Your window was open on account o' the steam heat hoppin' through the radiator too fast. Got that?"

Klein nodded. Then started fearfully as the door to the outer office was tried. Tried and knocked upon.

"Never mind that," said Cardinale. "You can say you didn't want to let anybody in till the cops came. I'll beat it like I came. Through the side door an' out through the Chief Clerk's office."

He walked around in front of Klein and fixed him with piercing black eyes. "Now get this. A guy called you up, see, an' made a date to meet you here in your office. He was comin' up with some red-hot dope for you, see. You came an' waited an' by-an'-by this guy shows up. You don't know him from Sweeney, see. He says he's gonna give you conviction-dope on a bootleggin' an' junk-pushin' outfit. You say O.K. an' there's no steno around so you get out a pencil an' pad an' get set to take down his statement, see."

Cardinale sniffed the air and turned off the fan. The knocking at the outer door had ceased.

He went on: "While you're gettin' set, he takes a turn over by the window an' you hear him mutter somethin' about, 'double-cross me, will they!' So you figure he's been gypped by a mob, see, an' that his dope'll be ace-high. Regular revenge stuff.

"You tell him to go ahead an' he turns around an' starts to say somethin' an'— Bing! Bing!—they get 'im from across the street, see. That's all. Just tell 'em your story an' go home. You're a Special Prosecutor and the D.A.'s flat on his back. You'll probably be in charge o' the investigation. But you can have a breakdown an' go to bed for a week on advice o' your physician. That'll knock the whole thing in the head an' by the end o' the week it'll be all washed up an' the papers 'll be full o' something else. Now don't forget your lines. I gotta hit the breeze."

"But the telephone call," said Klein. "What about that telephone call?"

"What telephone call?"

"The call that came just as you—er—just as the shots were fired."

"All right; I'll bite. What about it?"

Klein moistened dry lips with the tip of his tongue. "That was Harrigan," he said. "I'd stake my life that that was Harrigan."

"What if it was?"

Klein shook his head. "He's a devil, Cardinale! He's as cold as you are. He—he probably heard the shots! And why did he call just then? Do you suppose—"

Cardinale's thin lips were but a slash in his mask-like face. "You forget about Harrigan," he said. "I got plans for him."

"So have I, Cardinale," said a steely voice behind them.

Both men whirled. Klein sagged in his seat and grabbed at his heart with both hands. He wouldn't last through many like that. Cardinale's hand streaked half-way to his shoulder-holster—then halted.

The side door—the door to the Chief Clerk's office and the side stairs—had opened noiselessly. It stood half ajar and framed in the opening was the wiry form of Harrigan. In one hand was the ever-present cane; in the other a long, blued-steel .45 automatic. He said: "Sorry to interrupt, gentlemen, but you'll have plenty of time to finish the conversation. From the killing to the chair generally takes about a year."

Klein's voice was a hoarse whisper. "My ————! Oh, my ————!"

Cardinale said nothing. His slitted eyes narrowed still farther. He started to raise his hands.

"Hold it!" barked Harrigan. "Don't move!"

Cardinale shrugged and let his hands drop. His eyes bored into Harrigan's with a gaze that was almost hypnotic.

Harrigan's voice cracked like a whip. "Double your left hand into a fist and hold it straight out at your side."

Cardinale obeyed slowly.

"Now shake your arm."

Cardinale raised his eyebrows inquiringly. He said: "What'll I do next? Tell a funny story?" He shook his arm.

"Harder!" Harrigan's gun came up menacingly.

Cardinale snapped his arm obediently. A small revolver with its barrel sawed off about an inch from the cylinder jerked out of his sleeve and dangled on the end of a silver spring.

"That's better," said Harrigan—and pitched forward on his face.

Klein's eyes popped so you could almost hear 'em. Cardinale's sleeve-gun snapped into his hand. Around the corner of the door-jamb, slid Tony Martello, a short blackjack in his hand. He said: "It's us, Boss."

"An' about time!" said Cardinale.

MacFarlane came into the room behind Tony Martello.

"Take that," said Cardinale. He indicated the unconscious reporter. The two gangsters shouldered Harrigan and staggered out through the side office.

Cardinale picked up Harrigan's hat, cane and gun. He turned to Klein. He said: "Now don't get screwed up on your lines. An' stop worryin' about Harrigan. His ticket only calls for one-way transportation."

The door closed behind him.

HARRIGAN ROCKED IN a cradle of pain. To and fro—to and fro—back and forth. And with each pendulum-like swing, his agony increased....

He'd died and gone to hell and Cardinale and Klein had him tied on the end of a rope and were swinging him between them. And every time he swung close to them, they hit him on the head with Billy Sullivan's typewriter....

Funny how they'd gotten Sullivan's typewriter. He'd have to get hold of Klein and....

If he could only get off this damned rope. The swinging was driving him nuts....

With a great effort, Harrigan shook off his lassitude and roused himself. He swayed in the back seat of a rolling automobile. A wave of nausea swept over him. His head ached horribly; his stomach constricted; he retched.

"He's comin' out of it," said a voice, A voice that was miles away.

"Let 'im come. I got all the papers out of his pockets. If he had any dope written down, he won't have it when they pick him up."

Somebody laughed. A harsh, grating laugh that splintered against Harrigan's stiffened ear-drums with a jarring shock. The shock brought him back to earth.

He had a terrible head. Somebody must've been working it over with a cold-chisel. It'd been a long time since he'd been on a party like that....

He kept his eyes closed. Headaches always got worse if you opened your eyes. Not that this one could get any worse but the— Where had he been, anyway? He wished he could think of the name of the place so he'd be sure never to go there again....

A voice at his side said: "Drop me off a few blocks up. I'll catch a car an' straighten up an alibi. Later on, I may hafta get ahold o' Klein an' do a little master-mindin'."

Harrigan's sluggish pulses leaped. The rush of blood to his throbbing head doubled the agony. He almost fainted. But beyond the haze of pain was a clear-cut fact; that voice was the voice of Joe Cardinale and—suddenly—he remembered.

He'd had the biggest story in the history of the city right by the tail. He'd had the dope on the Sullivan killing. He'd been all set to send Cardinale to the chair and Klein to the pen and then—somebody'd socked him from behind! He wondered who it had been. If he kept still he'd probably find out…. Cardinale was speaking again.

"I haven't got time to go along on this. You guys know what to do. An' listen!"—Cardinale had a way of saying "LIS-sen!" that brought you up like the point of a bayonet. He said: "An' listen! No mistakes, see!"

"Don't worry," said a voice.

"Oke, Boss," said another.

Involuntarily, Harrigan's muscles tightened. Frank MacFarlane and Tony Martello! He was in nice company. He'd dreamed he was in hell and he hadn't been far wrong.

The car slid to a stop. Cardinale said: "Throw his hat an' cane alongside o' him. We don't care how soon they identify him." A door slammed.

The words seared into Harrigan's consciousness. Hell and all! He was being taken for a ride!

He sat up with a jerk and looked at the back of Frank MacFarlane's neck. MacFarlane was driving.

He turned his gaze slowly to the right. In the opposite corner of the back seat sat Tony Martello. Around his waist was a broad leather belt and attached to that belt was a sub-machine-gun. Its short nose was pointing inquisitively at Harrigan's stomach. In the seat between them lay hat, cane, cigarette-case and a couple of envelopes.

Harrigan glanced at the articles and hope tugged at his heart-strings. He was in a tough spot but there was still a chance. Set, in the head of that cane was a single-shot pistol of small caliber—a light, emergency gun.

He bowed ironically. "Good evening, Tonito mio."

Tony Martello grunted. He said: "Keep nice an' quiet, see." He moved the sub-machine-gun the merest trifle. The movement was suggestive.

Harrigan looked about him. The only light in the interior of the car came from the dim glow of the hooded dash-lamp. The shades were drawn but he could see forward through the windshield. The road was good but unfamiliar. The traffic was not heavy and the occasional lights were becoming more and more infrequent. He thought: "Another Long Island murder-mystery in the making."

Elaborately casual, he said: "It's a fine night for a murder, Tony."

Martello's sarcasm was supremely savage. He said: "Glad ya think so. 'S nice ta see a guy go out satisfied."

In the front seat, Frank MacFarlane snickered his appreciation of the grim jest.

Harrigan glanced at the speedometer strip. It hovered at thirty. That meant that they weren't clear of the city. They wouldn't knock him off yet!

He said: "I didn't know you were a wit, Tony. Service with a smile, is that it?" He rubbed his chin and, picking up his hat, stuck it on his head.

"Can that!" said Tony sharply. "I told ya not ta be makin' no unnecessary moves."

"You're a lousy host, Tony," said Harrigan dryly. "Anybody else'd tell a man to please himself in his last few minutes on this old ball o' mud."

"You'll have a long time ta please yourself when you get where you're goin'," rasped Tony Martello. "You do what I say, see!"

"Oh, go to hell," sighed Harrigan wearily. He picked up his cigarette-case and snapped it open.

In his corner, the fidgety machine-gunner snarled and stiffened. Harrigan half-expected the sub-machine to break into its deadly chatter. He was putting all his faith in that thirty-mile-an-hour speedometer reading. Somewhere back in misty memory, the voice of Joe Cardinale had said with savage emphasis: "An' listen! No mistakes, see!" And to machine-gun a man under the nose of a traffic-cop would be something of a mistake.

Harrigan, eyes fixed on the figures on the dashboard, selected a cigarette and lit it with a steady hand. Tony Martello did not fire.

The reporter dragged deeply on the cigarette and exhaled straight before him. In the poor light, the cloud of smoke completely hid Frank MacFarlane from his sight for a moment. Quickly, he veiled his eyes to hide the exultant gleam that he could not repress. Here was aid he had not counted on!

But his moment of triumph vanished as quickly as it came. The speedometer had jumped to thirty-five and his most important play was yet ahead of him. The play that he *must* get away with if he was to have his single desperate chance for life. His tone must be so cutting and his act so casual that Tony Martello would pay more heed to what he said than to what he did.

Contemptuously—with a sneer on his lips and an insult on his tongue—he turned to the slit-eyed killer who was his seat-mate.

"The trouble with a second-rate lush-roller like you, Tony, is that you've never been permitted to associate with gentlemen. You're just a punk and your place is in the back-room of a disorderly house. If you were anything except red-light scum, you'd know that a gentleman goes to his death as he goes to his dinner—unconcerned and fully clothed." His hand closed over the cane. "Now—why don't you shoot—rat!"

With a studied slowness, he turned his eyes from Tony Martello, placed the cane between his knees, rested his chin on the head of it and tensely awaited results.

But Tony Martello had been on rides before. In his eyes flickered little lights of amusement. The guy was getting tough—defying him. Next he'd be begging for his life—offering mythical millions to be let off. It always went like that—it was like a play. Tony awaited the next act in the comedy.

Harrigan, releasing his breath slowly as the momentary tension passed, twirled the head of his cane under his chin and glanced at the speedometer strip. It was moving... forty-five... forty-eight.... They were away from the city. It wouldn't be long now!

In his hand, held in its normal position, was the unscrewed head of the cane. He had one bullet—one shot—at his disposal. Should he try to beat Tony Martello to the trigger or should he beef MacFarlane and wreck the car? His glance went to the windshield.

Tony Martello's voice came to him. "Do the gentlemen that you're pally with know any prayers, guy?" The tone was bantering, confident.

Harrigan knew what it meant. He would turn his head to reply and look into a withering, wilting stream of lead. It would be the end! In the headlights, he caught a glimpse of trees and a winding, steeply banked road. His decision was made.

The cigarette dropped from his lips as he shot a great cloud of smoke from the side of his mouth. Back of it, his hand snapped up. A streak of flame burned across the back of the front seat. The light-control button shattered and buried itself in the dashboard. The lights went out and Harrigan dropped to the floor as a whirling stream of bullets sought him.

In the space of a split second, he jack-knifed his legs, shot forward and came up under Tony Martello's belt-gun. One hand grasped the already heating barrel of the gun; the other circled Tony's neck and brought his head down with a sudden jerk. Tony cursed—wrenched at his gun—tried to swing it free—but a steady pressure brought it up. His head, held in an iron grip—was forced lower and lower.

With a gasp, Tony saw his danger and pulled his thumb off the depressor. But the gun, forced from below, came up faster than his retreating arm and the trigger pressed firmly against the hand that he tried desperately to get out of the way. The barrel, resting almost under Tony's imprisoned chin, coughed once—twice—three times, and with a sobbing, choking: "Santa Maria!" Tony Martello died.

In the front seat, Frank MacFarlane plunged into sudden darkness, cursed and stamped on the brake. He made a frenzied grab for the light switch—found there wasn't any light switch there—ducked as a stuttering, whistling crescendo broke loose behind him—reached for the automatic under his arm and remembered—too late—that his car was rocking around a curve. Blindly, he swung the wheel, but his right front tire sheared off the gravel shoulder of the road and the big sedan started down.

MacFarlane was a good driver. Both feet braced against the

brake-pedal, he fought the bucking wheel. The sedan rocked, tottered, slid gently forward and hesitated on the brink of disaster. Then an arm slipped around MacFarlane's neck. His head was jerked backward in a strangling grip. He cried out— let go the wheel—and with a sudden rush, the great car took the plunge.

The sedan sailed through space, struck, bounced and sailed again. Inside, confusion was king. Glass shivered and jagged splinters whirred through the air. Metal twisted, shrieked and parted as bolts snapped and welding gave. Crash followed crash. The body of Tony Martello was hurled across Harrigan's straining legs. One of his threshing heels struck the dangling belt-gun and stinging bursts of flame stabbed through the blackness. Then, with a sound like a tearing tablecloth, the top opened and the trunk of a tree came in.

"IT'S THE LITTLE things in life," sang Irving Berlin. Harrigan, clinging grimly to the silver-chased robe-rack, was thrown on his back and hurled far forward. His head struck the wheel-post and snapping teeth sheared through the tip of his tongue. It was a lucky break. The sharp pain of that bitten tongue kept him from losing consciousness.

Dizzily, he crawled from under the dashboard. He spit a sweet-tasting crimson stream from his bitten tongue and wiped his mouth with the back of his hand. There was something in his hand. Instinctively, he knew that it was the rail of the robe-rack. His grip on it had been such that he'd taken it along with him.

Into the lesser blackness of a gaping hole that had once been a window, came the outline of a shaggy head. It was a head that wavered uncertainly—a groggy head—and, without hesitation, Harrigan swung his silver-plated piece of pipe. There was a sharp crack as metal and bone connected. Then with a sigh of escaping breath, the head disappeared. Came the noise of a body tumbling back into the wreckage and Harrigan mentally washed his hands of Frank MacFarlane.

He had quite a job to get out. There was a pain in the back of his head and his left leg didn't seem to want to behave. But he scrambled for the big hole opposite him. As he stepped across the seat his foot hit an inert body. That would be MacFarlane. Something occurred to him. He bent and fumbled for the armpit. From a shoulder-clip he lifted an enormously big and heavy gun. A young cannon. He stuck it in his pocket.

The ground swayed from under him as his feet struck it. He stumbled to his hands and knees and stayed there, shaking his head to clear it. One thing was certain—he had to get away from here....

He raised his head slowly and saw a reflection of light among the trees. Someone was coming.

He got up uncertainly. He was becoming accustomed to the darkness by this time and could see fairly well. On one side was the steep bank down which the sedan had hurtled; on the other, the smashed car and a few trees.

He scrambled up the bank and peered through the darkness at the opposite side of the road. There seemed to be more trees there and the cover was better. Lights were coming from both directions. He slipped into the shelter of the trees.

It was very dark. He stumbled and barked his shins and, here and there, were little patches of snow which chilled his feet. He didn't know where he was but he began to back-track the way he had come, keeping parallel to the road. In the distance, fixed lights glowed against the dark, threatening heavens.

Snarling like a machine-gun, the rapid exhaust of a motorcycle split the night. Harrigan saw the brilliant beam of its single eye and watched it coming. As it flashed by, the reflected light played on olive-drab and close-drawn parka. A trooper!

Harrigan rubbed the aching spot in the back of his head. He muttered: "Now where in hell am I?"

The simple thing—probably the correct thing—would be to go back, get himself identified with what had happened in the wrecked car, and be taken into custody. Then they'd take him to the Station and he could call the *Leader*. The *Leader* would rush him out of the hoosegow and into print. He'd write his story and call it a night.

Maybe!

For there were doubts. In Harrigan's mind ran the tail-end of the alibi that he had heard Cardinale frame for Klein as he stood in the Chief Clerk's office at Criminal Courts. It had been a nice alibi…. Too damned nice…. There was no reason to believe that they hadn't cinched him, too. Maybe, by this time, the cops and the *Leader* were looking for him as Sullivan's murderer. It wasn't impossible. Cardinale had said: "I got plans for Harrigan!" and what Joe Cardinale said, he generally meant.

And besides….

Harrigan was possessed of as fierce a pride as was Joe Cardinale. His vanity had been pricked. He had started on this story alone; he alone had all the inside dope; he alone knew what had really happened and he—alone—would bring it in.

Grimly, he trudged through bushes and leaves and patches of snow towards the lights in front of him.

His ultimate objective was Fifth Avenue in the Seventies. That was where Klein lived and Klein was the chink in Cardinale's armor. Klein had been an inadvertent witness to Sullivan's killing and now Cardinale needed Klein for a bit of plain and fancy perjury. By and by, Klein wouldn't be needed any more and when that time came, Klein would be hard to find.... Cardinale had a way with witnesses.

Klein, at Criminal Courts, had been useful to Cardinale. Klein, as witness to a murder, was still useful to Cardinale—for a time. If Harrigan could get to Klein before Cardinale did; if he could make the pressure sufficiently strong....

Harrigan, coming suddenly out from among the trees, spoke grimly aloud. He said: "I'll break the story or, by ———! I'll break Klein!"

He stood in an open space where the road widened and stretched into a sort of plaza. Before him were street-lights and signs in perforated tin.... New York.... White Plains.... Yonkers.... He must have been brought out along one of the parkways and not to Long Island. At the side of the road was a six-foot embankment and on top of that, lights, houses, a paved street, a parked Ford roadster with engine running.

Respect for persons and positions and property rights was just an idea to Harrigan. And Harrigan didn't take ideas seriously. There was no one on the street. Harrigan climbed the bank and walked quickly to the parked roadster. The running motor was swiftly explained. At the left of the driver's seat was a siren and on the door, the stenciled letters, "P.D."

Harrigan's reaction was worthy of Joe Cardinale. He looked at the siren's gaping maw, at the insignia of the Police Department on the door, murmured: "This'll be a quick trip!" and slammed home the rattling gears.

It was. He was hazy about the road but he stepped the accelerator to the floor and headed south. It wasn't long before he hit traffic and then—siren wailing and screaming—he was ascertaining just how fast a Ford roadster can negotiate Third Avenue's steel-studded length.

Clocked, his time would have been startling. Here and there, a policeman turned to stare after him and one or two headed for their patrol-boxes but none offered to stop him. The meaning shriek of his siren parted the traffic like a comb in a blonde wig. He swung crosstown past Madison, around an iron-staked enclosure into Fifth, and whirled along the edge of Central Park murmuring blessings on a city that numbers its streets and avenues so that he who runs may read.

He halted the car at the corner of the block and walked down the street. The fifth number was the mansion that Aaron Klein had built with crumbs from Cardinale's table. It was a low, massive affair with a glittering, gray-stone front. Long, polished windows, set in deep bays, were scattered across the face of it and the entrance and foyer were guarded by spear-shaped steel stakes, tipped with gold. If it had been situated on the Boston Post Road, automobiles would have stopped there for gasoline.

Harrigan knew the place like the potential housebreaker he was. When he had been after the proofs of collusion between politicians and food racketeers, he had fully determined to burglarize Klein's house and had studied it to that end. But Klein had seen the danger of exposure and turned up a couple of goats to take the fall. Harrigan had postponed his burglary. Well, he'd play a double-header now.

He walked to the end of the row of steel stakes and paused at the blind door of a street-level garage. The door had a lock; Harrigan already had a key; the two fitted admirably. He walked through the garage, out a side door and into a sort of screened courtyard. From around the corner of the house, he peered up at a rear second-floor window. A streak of light glinted from under a drawn curtain. Klein was in his study.

The reporter lowered his eyes. One of the dark, deeply set windows of the ground floor was directly opposite him. Swiftly, he leaped up into the embrasure. From a pocket in the rear lining of his coat came an ivory handled penknife and a short, stubby, blade snapped open. A peculiar blade that was tipped with a wheel. He selected a spot half-way up the lower pane and at the side of the window.

There was a faint crunching sound. The sound went on and on, then ceased abruptly, as Harrigan dropped the cutter and pressed both hands flat against the pane. It gave with a snapping click. For an instant, it tottered against the heavy curtain and in that instant Harrigan's darting hand came through the hole it had left, caught it, drew it gently outward and laid it on the broad cement ledge.

Harrigan was slim and the pane, though narrow, was long. Carefully avoiding the wired window-frame, he stepped into the room. He crossed the thick rug, opened a door gently, went through another room, crossed a vaulted hall and started up a wide marble staircase. He had no fear of servants; none of them slept in the house. Klein had strange visitors at strange hours and prying domestics might become expensive.

Aaron Klein sat at his desk, his head bowed in his hands. It came up with a jerk as Harrigan entered the room. The sight was no tonic. His mouth opened; his eyes widened; he seemed to try to shrink within himself; he was mortally afraid. He raised his hands in a feeble gesture of self-protection and his slack lips mouthed the inevitable: "My ———!"

"Not yet," said Harrigan; "but soon!" From his right hand dangled Frank MacFarlane's giant gun and on his face was a grimace of disgust. He walked across the room and prodded the limp, fat figure with the muzzle of the gun. "Come on!" he said. "Snap out of it!"

Klein mumbled incoherently. He was almost in the last stages of physical fear.

Harrigan prodded him again. "All right," he said. "Cut out the blubbering. It won't do you any good. I think I'll kill you anyway. Shoot you down in cold blood like you did Billy Sullivan."

"I—I—I did-didn't s-s-shoot Sullivan!" gasped Klein.

"You didn't have the nerve, that's the only reason. You did the dirty work; put him on a spot in your office!"

"I didn't!" moaned Klein. "I swear to ———"

"He's tired of being sworn at," snapped Harrigan. His voice rasped again: "Don't waste any more time, you louse! Come through! Who killed Sullivan and why? And your name signed to it." The gun swung up, threateningly.

Klein took a desperate grip on himself. He spoke as one who repeats a well-learned but meaningless lesson. "Sullivan came to my office with a story about some racketeers who had double-crossed him—"

Harrigan's voice was a breath of the Antarctic. "I'll give you one more chance, Klein. How'd the kid come to stumble over a snake like you?"

Klein's eyes were fixed on space. His hands were clenched at his sides. His voice was toneless. He began, "Sullivan had been racketeering for—" He shrieked as the double sights of the heavy gun cut a ragged, crimson furrow across his lardy face.

He cowered in his chair moaning, crying and dabbing at his face while the dread voice—the voice of death—poured into his cringing ears.

"One more crack about young Sullivan racketeering and I'll gun-whip your face to a hamburg! When you're past human suffering, I'll kill you!" The gun dug into the layers of greasy fat that surrounded Klein's neck. "You've been in on a lot o' killin' in your time, Klein. In a couple o' seconds, you're gonna be in on a little more. Comin' through?"

Klein's voice was thick and his tongue played him tricks. The words were barely audible. "Cardinale killed him!"

"Yeah. An' the Allies won the war. Why'd Sullivan come to your office? What'd he have that incriminated you? Quick!" The threatening gun-barrel jerked past Klein's bulging eyes, hung over his face for an instant and started down.

Klein ducked and covered his face with his hands. "A fountain pen!" he screamed. "A fountain pen with my name on it! It's in my desk at Criminal Courts!" He couldn't get the words out fast enough.

"And it's got a nice set o' Cardinale's prints on it," said Harrigan. "And it carries an explosive bullet. Just a nice little fountain-pen gun!"

He straightened and slid the gun into his hip pocket. He said: "One look at Harms' carcass ought to have explained the mystery. An' I didn't see it. I'm gettin' old an' dumb. I ought to get a bullet in my rump!"

"Don't worry; you will!" It was Joe Cardinale's most matter-of-fact tone.

HARRIGAN'S JAWS CAME together with a click. His hands knotted into fists and his whole body went rigid. He sucked air through his teeth with a hissing noise. He thought: "I'm in a hell of a mess now!"

One thumb hooked in a lower vest-pocket, he turned slowly on his heel. His mouth was wry—derisive. He said: "So your whole mob 're gum-shoe artists now, eh?"

Cardinale paid no attention. He stood just inside the door. A black cigar-butt was clenched between his teeth and a blacker gun was leveled from his hip. His eyes were on Harrigan but his words winged at Klein.

He said: "You lousy punk! You lousy, yellow, skirt-bullyin' punk!"

On Klein's face was a strange expression. An expression that was a curious mixture of great relief and still greater fear. He followed the direction of Cardinale's gaze and shot a look of venomous hatred at Harrigan. He said: "That's right, Joe. I stalled him till you came. Let him have it! He's a ————" The rest was obscenity.

Cardinale laughed noiselessly. A queer man with a queer sense of humor, the situation amused him. Without taking his eyes from Harrigan, he said: "It's *you* I'm talkin' to, you greasy little rat! I heard how you stalled him. You yelled it so loud you woke up two cops in Canarsie."

Klein jerked in his chair as though he'd caught a bullet. His face was like unleavened dough. His voice was a pitiful whine. "I did it to warn you, Joe! I swear to ———— I did! I heard you come up the stairs and—"

"I didn't come up the stairs," said Cardinale evenly. He spit out the cigar-butt. "Come over here, Klein."

Klein, hesitant but incapable of disobedience, shuffled slowly towards him.

"Stop!" said Cardinale. "Right there."

Klein stopped. He was at one side of Harrigan and somewhat farther forward.

"That's fine," said Cardinale. "Now I can watch this reporter-guy while I'm stickin' a slug in you." The gun moved just a trifle.

"Me! Me!" Klein was screaming. "Joe! Joe! For the love of ————!" He was on his knees, hands extended, palms up.

Cardinale's mask-like features relaxed into what was almost a smile. Without looking at the kneeling supplicant, he said: "Make the act real good, Punk, an' I might let you live an extra five minutes."

There was a rubbing, shuffling sound as Klein began to crawl towards the killer on his knees.

"Joe!" he sobbed. "Joe!"

Again, Cardinale shifted the gun a trifle. Then came a choking gurgle, an exclamation, a wheeze of escaping breath, and a body struck the floor heavily.

Neither of the two men who faced each other across the room, looked towards the sound. Their eyes bored into each other. It was almost a mutual hypnosis.

"Looks like I saved a bullet," said Cardinale. "He's damn' little a pound, now."

"Yeah," said Harrigan; "he had a bum clock an' when it saw you, it stopped altogether."

Both were rigid—unmoving. Cardinale was leaning a trifle

forward, gun angling up from the hip. He said: "Where's Martello an' MacFarlane?"

Harrigan was back on his heels, legs sagging a bit at the knees. The thumb of his right hand was lying along the edge of his lower vest-pocket. The fingers were spread and hooked like the talons of a bird of prey. He said: "If White Plains has got a morgue, they're in it."

Cardinale's eyes were opaque. He said: "They'd better be." He came up on the balls of his feet. His knuckles whitened around the grip of the gun. The black eyes glittered a warning. The gun started up.

Harrigan's thumb slid away from the pocket. Then, with a swift motion it swooped downward to the butt of the gun on his hip.

Cardinale read the danger of that flashing hand. He hurried his shot.

He need not have feared. Frank MacFarlane had never relied on speed of hand and his gun-barrel wasn't stripped. The front sight caught in the lining of Harrigan's pocket and, far from beating Cardinale to the trigger, he was clearly beaten.

Cardinale had meant to stop Harrigan's clock. Instead, the hurried shot broke his left shoulder. It whirled him completely around and dropped him to his knees and Joe's second bullet parted his hair as he fell. Then Harrigan's gun was loose and his right hip erupted in a geyser of flame and lead.

Cardinale felt the walls of his stomach cave inward and knew that he was through. His third shot bored through the floor at his feet as he pitched forward. His gun slipped from nerveless fingers and fell to the carpet.

From flat on his face, he edged himself upward. Shirt and

coat were dyed with crimson; blood trickled from both corners of his mouth. Lips drawn back in a jungle snarl, he propped his shattered body on an elbow. His hand groped claw-like for the long-barreled automatic.

Harrigan, in the act of climbing to his feet, slipped back on his heels and fired again. The automatic spun away from Cardinale's straining fingers and thudded against the wall behind him. Cardinale's grasping hand went limp. His nostrils distended and shot out a stream of blood. His eyes flickered and shut. His head dropped forward on his chest.

Harrigan staggered to his feet. He drew a long breath and grasped his left hand by the wrist. He raised it and thrust the hand into his coat pocket. It would do as an improvised sling. The operation took him two full minutes. He groaned and the sweat rolled from his face in great drops.

He went to the door, locked it, set a chair under the knob and looked at the clock on the desk. Twenty-two minutes to go for the Late Edition! Well, they'd have to knock off the front page, that's all. To hell with the time!

His arm hurt like the devil. He sat down at the desk, wondered how fast a busted shoulder bleeds and picked up the telephone. He said: "Gimme Barclay 9-7000."

The Managing Editor could not be spoken to. He was busy—he was out—he was sorry—

"Snap out of it, baby. This's Harrigan."

Baby snapped out of it. The M.E. was on the wire in a twinkling.

"Yes—yes! What is it?"

"It's Harrigan. I'm at Aaron Klein's house. Cardinale's cashed and so's Klein. An' plenty others. Get set down there. I'm gonna knock everythin' off the wrapper except the date-line!"

"Wait! Wait!"

He heard the M.E. shout for a stenographer. He heard him roar for the stopping of the presses. Then: "Let 'er rip, Harrigan!"

Harrigan let 'er rip. He had an awful pain in his busted shoulder. His eyes were closing. He wanted to sleep—to smoke—to do any damned thing except sit motionless before that phone. But he sat and words dripped from his lips and fell into the gaping transmitter in an uninterrupted stream.

There came an imperative rattle of a club on the door.

"Open up in there! Police!"

"Don't need a cop," shouted Harrigan. "Get a couple undertakers," and went on dictating his story.

A body crashed against the panels. Again; and again. The door shivered, splintered and caved inward with a crash. Six policemen menaced Harrigan with drawn revolvers. He hung up the receiver, sighed and grinned crookedly.

"Something I can do for you, boys?"

Kick-Back

*Harrigan takes a 24 carat shellacking for
a beat, and then gets only a kick-back*

FRANCIS ST. XAVIER HARRIGAN—star reporter, deadly gunman, from earlier occupation—lolled at his desk in the *Leader* office and slept dull care away.

The telephone snarled in his ear. Harrigan shook his head a little, wet dry lips with the tip of his tongue and settled deeper into the chair.

The telephone continued to ring. Harrigan roused, shoved his hat on the back of his neck and cursed the newspaper business. He picked up the receiver; said ironically: "Well, who's dead now?"

A man's voice, very low, said: "Nobody—yet!"

The fog of sleep lifted from Harrigan's brain. There was something personal in that crack. He asked: "Why—is somebody going to be?"

The same voice, thick and muffled, came again. "That's liable to be up to you, brother. It's your move. Frank Crocker's gunnin' for you!"

Harrigan came upright in his chair. The ends of his mustache came down in a sneer. Frank Crocker gunning for him? Good; he had a long score to settle with rats of the Crocker breed! Questions rattled in his throat. "Where is he? And who are you?"

The voice answered, "He's in the Myer Building. 1413, I think. You better duck. You asked for it in this morning's paper an' don't be surprised if you get it. Me—I'm just a friend. Thought I'd tip you off."

Harrigan's lips twisted. He said: "Thanks, friend; but you're wasting your time. You better warn Crocker. If that louse makes a play for me, he'll get hit with Chicago lightning!"

"Yeah!" There was a sneer in the muffled tone. "That kid, Sullivan, was a wiseguy too, an' look what happened to him!" The receiver clicked sharply.

Harrigan cursed and left the office in nothing flat.

HIGH UP IN the Myer Building, Frank Crocker quivered in the throes of rage. His hundred and eighty pounds were a bundle of raw nerves. He cursed and was silent by turns. The most important play of his career was in danger of going wrong.

Spread on the desk in front of him, lay the morning's *Leader*. Black headlines glared up at him. For perhaps the twentieth time, he re-read them. *"Political Conspiracy Exposed. Kane-Crocker Tie-Up Hinted. Racketeer May Be Backing Reform Candidate."*

A flood of obscenities burst from his lips anew and his dark eyes flashed again to the by-line. *"By F. St. X. Harrigan, Leader Staff Correspondent."* With passionate earnestness, he consigned Frank Harrigan to the lowest pit of hell.

A door at the end of the room opened and Icky Yeager, Frank Crocker's chief of strafe, came in.

They presented a sinister picture as they stood beside the desk. The flat, un-muscled tautness of Icky Yeager was the tautness of a coiled snake; the blue sheen of Frank Crocker's close-shaven jowl was the dull blue of an automatic pistol. One short and stocky, the other thin and anaemic, they had a quality in common—both radiated danger.

Icky Yeager dropped words into the silence. "How much d'you figure this Harrigan knows?"

"How the hell do I know?" snapped the politician. "That's what I got to find out! An' I can't wait to read it in the paper, either!"

The gunman's eyes were cold and hard. He rubbed his right hand gently over his left lapel. He said significantly: "When he comes in we'll find out what he knows!"

Frank Crocker stopped him with raised hand. "Not that way," he said quickly. "I don't want trouble if I can side-step it. It's damn' close to election an' dead men don't make good campaign-posters."

"Then, how—"

The politician made a sweeping gesture of impatience. "Don't do so damn' much worryin'," he growled. "I gotta figure out the play. Get outside and let me think!"

Icky Yeager shrugged and went out through the door to the outer office. Frank Crocker sat down at the desk, put his mind on his problem, his elbows on the *Leader* and began to stroke his hair.

Fourteen floors below him, Eighth Avenue seethed and swirled. Through the high windows of his office-apartment, the distant Hudson gleamed coldly. Across the flat mahogany desk, "Ape" Scalisi—half an inch from eyebrow to hairline, half a yard around the biceps—was shoving two closely figured ledger sheets. He was saying: "Here's the latest figgers on the Kane campaign dough, Boss. Yeager brung 'em in but he forgot to give 'em to you. Too excited over that damn' rat down to the *Leader!*"

To none of this, Frank Crocker paid any attention. His wide-set, level eyes stared into space. His broad forehead was furrowed and lined. His mane of very black hair gleamed like burnished ebony from the constant passing of his hand over it.

Ape Scalisi hesitated; asked: "Anythin' you want, Boss?" waited a moment and went back into the outer office, closing the door behind him.

Frank Crocker heeded neither question nor movement. He wrestled with his problem. And Crocker was a good wrestler. At least, he had been. Prizefighter and bartender, too. And high-class procurer.

A guy like that is a natural. His course is plainly marked. Frank Crocker took to politics like a Kerry man to a brick.

Not that he ran for office. Hell, no! Frank Crocker cared nothing for who made the City's laws; he wanted to make its law-makers. He had money, which he spent; underworld connections, which he used; a golden smile that shone over everything.

From racketeer to political power is a short step anywhere. Frank Crocker's case was no exception. His name began to mean something. Politicians bowed to him; Police-sergeants waved at him; newspapers gave him feature stories. But Frank Crocker wasn't satisfied.

He was broad without being squat and heavily muscled without being beefy. He had a jaw that was built along the delicate lines of the front end of a steam-roller and he had one great ambition: To control the office of Mayor of the City of New York. He wasn't so far away!

And then the bottom fell out of the bag.

Front-page scandals had leaked. Civic corruption had been exposed. John Voter was running a temperature. The political line-up changed over-night. A reform ticket came into the field.

Reform tickets are like Broadway tryouts. They'll give the public a good run for somebody else's money.

Frank Crocker saw the chance of a life-time. Much money appeared from nowhere. The Reform Ticket began to boom. Monster rallies were held. John Voter was shouting: "Down with Corruption!"

The ticket was, in the main, a good one. The newspapers picked it up and shoved it along. More money came and, with it, more publicity. A wave of hysteria swept the city. Father Knickerbocker's house-cleaning was on.

And back of Ezra Kane, candidate for President of the Board of Aldermen, stood Frank Crocker—anonymous as a selling-plater—a money-bag in each hand.

The situation shaped beautifully. The fatal Tuesday was very close. The newspapers were solid in support and the Reform Ticket was even money. No one suspected phenagling. Frank Crocker was getting along.

And then, with election a week away, Harrigan of the *Leader* broke a headline over his skull.

It was a stunning wallop, but Frank Crocker had ridden many a K.O. punch. He leaned his elbows on the desk, muttered: "This guy will have to be taken care of!" and began to stroke his sable mane.

His elbows rumpled paper. He looked down. His darkly frowning eyes fell on the two neatly figured sheets of the expenditures for Ezra Kane's campaign. They totaled a staggering sum but he scarcely glanced at it. He took a fountain pen from his vest-pocket, scrawled: "O.K. Frank Crocker," across the lower right-hand corner of each sheet; said: "Harrigan, eh!" and stabbed a savage period.

He laid the Okeyed accounts at one side of the desk, folded the *Leader* over them and placed a paperweight on everything. He thought: "It's damn' close to election to knock him off, but—"

He looked up suddenly as the knob to the door of the outer office was tried. Came a shout—the sound of running feet—the thud of a falling body. The stillness was shattered by a great roar of pain and rage.

Frank Crocker left his chair like Dempsey used to leave his corner.

He flung open the door to the outer office. There Harrigan, the despised reporter, and Ape Scalisi were engaged in a merry-go-round.

There was a growing lump on Scalisi's bullet-head where Harrigan's cane might have contacted; but right now Harrigan was fast becoming the underdog. Long, tenuous arms were round him. His arms were pinned to his sides. A huge hand fumbled for his throat.

Harrigan writhed and gasped for breath. He could not free his arms. He twisted his head sidewise. A thumb brushed across his parted lips. He opened his mouth and let the thumb come in. Then his jaws locked like the leaves of a steel trap.

Scalisi roared like a wounded bull. The fingers of his right hand clawed at Harrigan's eyes. His left arm circled the reporter's waist in a bone-crushing grip. Harrigan was bent backward to the breaking point. His ribs caved, his knees buckled, black spots danced before his eyes.

Then the voice of Frank Crocker cried: "Break! Break! What the hell is this, anyway!"

HARRIGAN HAD DANTE stopped. He'd go to hell for a story, too—and get back in time for the late edition. He hunted headlines and the underworld was his hunting ground. Yeggs and racketeers were his meat; and crooked politicians. He pursued and they dodged and sometimes they sniped at him from ambush. It was a sort of a game and Harrigan didn't mind—until they murdered Billy Sullivan.

Sullivan'd been a nice kid. Harrigan had liked him a lot; had taken him under his wing and practically adopted him. But the kid had dug up a big killing and the rats had bumped him off. And tried to frame him.

Harrigan had smashed the frame; more, he'd gotten the kid's killer. But that hadn't cleared the slate. The bitterness remained. No longer, was "getting the news" an exciting game between crooks and himself. It was now a battle in deadly earnest with Harrigan striving to lay gangdom bare—to expose every crooked move to the newspaper-reading public.

And now he had come to the front line trenches again, and moved over No Man's Land into enemy territory.

Frank Crocker sat down at his desk and crossed his legs. Ape Scalisi went out and shut the door. Harrigan drew a handkerchief from his breast-pocket and dabbled at a bloodied lip. He said: "Good bodyguard, Scalisi. But he takes his work too seriously."

Frank Crocker lit a black cigar and spoke between the puffs: "You got plenty Moxie to come bustin' in here like this."

"Why?" Harrigan's eyes were innocent. "You wanted to see me, didn't you?"

Frank Crocker took the cigar from his mouth; asked in a surprised tone: "What makes you think that?"

Harrigan shrugged; asked: "What'd you have Yeager call me for and tell me where you were if you didn't want to see me?"

Frank Crocker's lips were hard and straight. He said something under his breath.

Harrigan laughed, dabbed at his lips with his handkerchief, replaced it; said: "Don't give Icky too much hell about this. I was just guessing. And you've confirmed the guess."

Frank Crocker's eyes reflected a savage humor. He hurled the cigar into a brass cuspidor, sat up straight at the desk; said through tight lips: "Listen here. You're just too damned clever to live! But I can't be havin' trouble now. It's too close to election. If you'll play dead an' keep your nose clean till the votes are counted, I'll cut you in for five grand."

Harrigan grinned. "You throw your dough around like a Prohi on a party. The reform-racket must be a moneymaker."

Frank Crocker rasped: "I knew damn' well you'd chisel for more. But you won't get it! Five grand is tops. It's a lot o' dough for a minor political office."

Harrigan's eyes toyed with the angry figure before him. "Minor political office," he mimicked. His tone was suddenly crisp. "What the hell d'you mean—minor? You're running Kane for President of the Board, aren't you? Well, if something should happen—and something will!—to the duly elected mayor of this fair city, who'd be mayor, huh? Right; the President of the Board of Aldermen! And Frank Crocker'd own him! Pretty sweet, eh?"

Crocker's heavy face was impassive. His lips were stiff. His eyes were disks of flint. His voice grated: "I'm givin' your lousy, snoopin' hide a break. You can take it or leave it!"

Harrigan smiled; said softly: *"Reporter Scorns Bribe. Racketeer's Power Broken.* What a lead for the early edition!"

Frank Crocker's mask gave way. His mouth was an ugly gash. He snarled: "There's no early edition in hell!" He jabbed a button; jabbed again.

The door to the outer office opened and Ape Scalisi came in. The door at the end of the room flew back and Icky Yeager stood on the threshold. Both held leveled guns.

Harrigan's face was hard as granite. He bit his wounded lip. The blood began to flow afresh. He said: "Stuck-o!"

Frank Crocker leaned back in his chair and sneered. "I gave you a break an' you muffed it. You can have it now—in the neck!" The gunners started forward.

Blood oozed down over Harrigan's chin. He put his hand to his breast-pocket slowly. The advancing gunmen tensed. A hammer went back with a metallic click. He drew out the handkerchief and swabbed at his lip.

He bent close to Frank Crocker. His voice was low and cold. "It's too close to election for gunplay, you fool!"

"I know," said Crocker, "but it's easier to fight fancy than fact. Pick your spot, wiseguy!"

There was a pressure on Harrigan's kidneys. Icky Yeager, dapper and dangerous, spoke: "Oke, brother. Loft 'em. High!"

Frank Crocker, dark eyes locked with the reporter's gray ones, leaned back in his chair and watched Harrigan replace his bloody handkerchief. Harrigan's voice was bantering. "Will you have it here or in Mineola?"

Frank Crocker gasped and went suddenly rigid.

Harrigan's hand had dug deep in his breast-pocket; passed through a cunningly split seam to the gun in his shoulder-holster. A blued-steel .45 automatic was level. Frank Crocker was staring straight up Death Alley.

He recoiled, gasped: "Wait—"

Icky Yeager's gun bored into Harrigan's back. Ape Scalisi was two feet away to the left. Harrigan held Frank Crocker with an almost hypnotic gaze.

The politician was stiff as a corpse. The barrel of the automatic nuzzled into his neck. Harrigan's words were like tinkling, musical notes running the blazing scale of death. "We're gambling for real stakes now, Crocker! And it'll be damned close! Go ahead—deal!"

Frank Crocker's face was a dirty gray. He gagged convulsively; said nothing.

At Harrigan's left, Ape Scalisi bent at the knees and flexed one long arm at his side. At Harrigan's right, a reaching arm pressed lightly against him as Icky Yeager swung round to break his wrist. The steel spring gave a little as Harrigan's finger went tight on the trigger. By ———! he wouldn't go out alone!

In front of him, Frank Crocker came out of his nearly fatal trance. "Don't!" he cried in a strangled tone. "Lay off, you dummies! Down rods!"

Scalisi and Yeager drew back and lowered their guns. Harrigan straightened and laughed—a high-pitched, unnatural laugh. Frank Crocker went limp in his chair and the sweat streamed off his face. The portals of death had gaped.

Harrigan stepped slowly around Frank Crocker. He gestured with the gun. "Come on," he said. "Let's go. I want to get out of here."

Crocker wiped sweat from his forehead. "Go on," he said. "Nobody's stopping you."

Harrigan grinned a twisted grin. "Maybe not, but you're coming out to the elevators with me." He took the folded *Leader* from Crocker's desk, covered his gun-hand with it and prodded the political boss to his feet. He said: "I wouldn't trust you as far as Primo Carnera sways in the breezes. Come on!"

At the elevators, he rang the bell, watched Frank Crocker turn and reenter the office. He crushed the *Leader* in his hand and took the stairs, half a landing at a jump.

In the office, Ape Scalisi opened and shut tremendous hands. The thumbs were almost as long as the fingers. He asked: "Will we go get 'im, Boss?"

Frank Crocker snapped: "Certainly; go get him!" He turned to the desk, grew suddenly pale; gasped: "——— ———!"

Scalisi and Yeager wheeled in their tracks; asked simultaneously: "Whatsa matter, Boss?"

"Matter!" roared Frank Crocker. "Matter? Damn his stinkin' soul, he's got the Kane campaign account! An' I Okeyed and signed it! Come on; quick!"

HARRIGAN CAME INTO Forty-third Street like a breeze from a swinging door. He knew that pursuit would follow fast but a minute's start was enough. Once in that tangle of traffic, he'd be as safe as the gold reserve. He saw a taxi, beckoned to it; snapped: "Leader Square, fast!" and settled back to light a cigarette.

The cigarette-case had a mirror set in its cover. In the mirror, Harrigan caught a glimpse, through the side window, of three men boiling into Forty-third Street from the lobby of the Myer Building.

Harrigan thought: "Damn' quick work!" and watched them climb into a car. He watched them gesticulating; knew that they had seen him. In every direction, a wall of moving traffic stretched. There was no chance to slip away unnoticed.

He watched through the mirror as they closed in, then rapped on the glass and said to the driver: "See that Duplex behind us?"

The driver looked in his mirror and nodded.

Harrigan barked: "Lose it!"

The driver nodded easily and wheeled into the thickest of the traffic, looking for a break. He got it, shot through a momentary opening and was off, zig-zagging between the El pillars. He turned left—through a one-way street—right, through a shopping center; hit the inside lane of fast traffic, stepped the gas down to the floor and slid past a cop in the act of raising his hand to halt the flow of vehicles. He saw an opening, passed a trolley on the wrong side, turned right again and swung into the motor-maze of one of New York's most heavily trafficked arteries. The Duplex was right behind.

The driver—his name on the card was Marx—looked in the mirror, grunted; said: "He don't lose so easy, does he?"

Harrigan, leaning forward and bending low in the seat, spoke to the back of the driver's head. "A double-sawbuck if you get to Leader Square without him."

Chauffeur Marx turned his head a little, cast a swift glance of appraisal over his fare; asked cautiously: "You said a *double* sawbuck, mister?"

"Right! Can you do it?"

The driver's answer was a chuckle. He straightened behind the wheel and pulled his cap over his eyes. "For twenty bucks, mister, I could lose a Mack truck on a miniature golf course!"

The hide-and-go-seek was on. It was a beautiful game. Both men had apparently been born with steering wheels in their hands. They beat lights, timed signals, judged the gestures of the traffic cops with the accuracy of striking snakes. They were Wizards of the Wheel—Masters of the Machine—typical New York taxi drivers.

For twenty blocks, they dived and dodged and neither gained an inch. Harrigan was crouched low in the seat lest Frank Crocker, growing desperate, should order Icky Yeager to shoot. Then at Twenty-fourth Street, Harrigan's driver swung into a lane between parallel lines of traffic. The Duplex, with nowhere else to go, followed him in. The taxi began to slow—to diminish speed—to loaf along in the ebb of the traffic. Harrigan looked up in alarm. His hand went inside his coat.

The Twenty-third Street light was dying. The taxi crawled on. Horns began to blow, brakes squealed, drivers cursed. The Duplex nosed out to come alongside. Harrigan drew his gun. The light went red.

The traffic officer's whistle shrilled. Marx flashed his stop-light, slid gently over the cross-walk and came to an abrupt halt in the patch of the crosstown traffic.

The policeman's face was a classic in disgust. He roared: "Hey, there! Where d'ye think y'are, you dimwit! Get back!"

But the Duplex had blocked the gap. There was no space to retreat. The crosstown traffic was closing in. The taxi had several cars blanketed. The air quivered with the raucous sound of horns.

The officer ground his teeth. He was fed up with bonehead drivers. His voice was hoarse; his face was red. He cried: "You damned mopey half-wit! I'll give you a ticket to Bellevue!" He started towards the taxi. A horn blared in back of him. He jumped; grated:

"My ————! if I only had time!"

He halted the traffic momentarily; roared: "Get out o' here, you sleepy dope, before I lose me temper!" He waved the taxi through. The driver grinned; Harrigan sighed; the crosstown traffic closed behind them like a wave.

At Twenty-second, Marx swung west on an east-bound street, went twenty feet, swung completely around in a maze of cursing drivers and headed back into the avenue from which he had come.

Harrigan clenched his fists and swore. "What a dumb play! You lost all you gained, you wooden-head!"

"Yeah?" said the driver. "Look behind you."

Harrigan looked. The Duplex was gone.

The driver grinned at his puzzlement. "That's the break I wanted," he explained. "A block's lee-way an' a right turn. Soon's I turned, he did—goin' over to cut me off. I'll drift along a few blocks an' swing crosstown. By that time, he'll be comin' back to look for me. I'll see 'im no more today."

"Smart boy!" said Harrigan. "That rates an extra ten."

The cabby grinned. "Ride often, Mister!" he said.

The taxi drifted on. Three blocks went past. Harrigan took his hand away from his gun, settled back in the seat, sighed— and went out like a match in the wind.

HARRIGAN LAY IN the street with his back to an El pillar. He spit out a mouthful of blood and began to sit up and take notice.

A small crowd had already gathered and more people were adding themselves to it. Between the curb and the trol-ley-tracks, the taxi leaned drunkenly on its nose. It was spew-ing oil and steaming water. The big Duplex, sweeping in from Eighteenth Street, had cut it almost in half.

A large policeman, note-book and pencil in hand, was barg-ing up, asking questions as he came. A muscular, well-set-up man with a mane of very black hair moved close to him and spoke in low tones. He pulled the engraved card of a political club from his pocket and showed it to the policeman. He said:

"I am Frank Crocker, Officer, and I feel that this crash is largely my fault. I told my driver to hurry and this is the result. I feel responsible for the safety of these men and I want to get them to a hospital as quickly as possible so that they can get medical aid without delay. The car I was riding in is in good condition and my driver is not hurt. Can you oblige me by letting me take them, right away?"

The cop twisted the pasteboard in his fingers. He knew the name—who didn't? knew that it was synonymous with great political power. He cleared his throat nervously. He was in a tough spot. He had his duty to do and he wanted to do it—but not in Staten Island. He took his courage in both hands; said hesitatingly: "Why—yes—Mr. Crocker, but—er—my report—"

Frank Crocker stopped him with raised hand. "Certainly, Officer; certainly! Make out your report in the usual way, by all means! You may report me as responsible for the entire occurrence. All I want is permission to take these unconscious men to a hospital without having to wait for an ambulance. I shall consider it a great favor, Officer."

The officer sighed and looked relieved. Failure to call an ambulance, would be—at worst—a minor irregularity. He said: "Okey, Mr. Crocker. That'll be fine," and turned again to his note-book.

Harrigan, collecting his scattered wits with an effort, began to realize that all was far from fine. He put a hand against the El pillar, started to raise himself; cried: "Hey! Just a—"

Ape Scalisi, above and behind him, spread an overcoat in protective fashion and parted his hair with the butt of a .38. Harrigan sighed a little and went into the clear without a murmur.

A man in a brown top-coat, standing on the other side of the pillar, had a clear view. His eyes widened. Color flooded his face. He took a sudden step forward and cried: "Officer! Officer! I saw—"

Icky Yeager, cool and deadly, fell negligently into step with him. His right hand was in his top-coat pocket and the pocket flap was slightly raised. From under it, a blued-steel, octagonal barrel peered questioningly into the world.

The officer, pencil poised, turned quickly about. "Well," he asked: "What did you see?"

The indignant citizen halted in mid-stride. The hole in that blued-steel barrel was staring him straight in the eye. The color drained from his face as suddenly as it had come. He gulped, wet parched lips, made aimless gestures with his hands. High resolve fell from him. He mumbled: "I saw the accident, Officer."

The policeman sighed and shook his head. He said, ironically: "You an' the other six million!" and turned again to his notes.

Frank Crocker was saying: "Let's not waste any more time, Officer. These men may be seriously injured."

"Okey, Mr. Crocker," said the cop, and started towards the taxi. Frank Crocker beckoned with raised finger.

Ape Scalisi caught the sign. He picked Harrigan up like a bag of meal and slammed him into the Duplex. He and the big policeman took the unconscious Marx from behind the wheel of the wrecked taxi. Frank Crocker was going over the cab, picking up scattered articles.

The cop stepped into the Duplex, laid Marx's shoulders on the rear seat, and started to back out on the far side. The door slammed behind him. A sharp object jabbed him at the waistline. Icky Yeager's voice was low in his ear: "No reportin' for you, Cull! We're takin' you along."

Frank Crocker, shutting his own door, murmured: "If you

don't mind." Ape Scalisi, leaning back through the front window, held a Colt .38 very low. He said: "He damn' well better mind!"

The Duplex, leaking a little oil, roared crosstown.

HARRIGAN CAME OUT of the ether by sections. He was damnably cold and he creaked all over. The back of his head was the worst. It was noisier than an Elks' clambake.

He tried to put his hands to his head—discovered that he couldn't; tried to sit up—found he couldn't do that either. He started to swear—got only bubbling noises. He was bound—hand and foot—and gagged. He thought: "I can still see; wonder how they overlooked that," and began to take stock of his surroundings.

He was stretched on a low, hard cot, almost under a window. The cot was pushed close to the wall. At the bottom of the window was a partly open transom. A cold wind blew in.

Late sunlight glinted across the transom, making its lower face a reflector. A broad street—high-stooped houses—trolley-tracks—automobiles—going in both directions. Yet the picture in the glass was a silent one. Now and then, a horn blared faintly; a street-car went past with scarcely a sound; the unceasing flow of human voices was not to be heard at all.

Harrigan, his numbed brain awakening, strained his ears to catch the familiar noises. He couldn't be far above the street; why didn't the street-sounds come to his ears? The explanation burst on him suddenly. He was in a sound-proof room. That was why the transom was open; they didn't want him to smother! He thought: "They're damned careful to keep me alive. I must be worth something to 'em."

He twisted his head towards the interior of the room and saw a startling picture. On the floor, in the corner opposite the couch, a big man lay trussed and gagged. A man as tall as himself and half again as heavy. A man in blue clothes and brass buttons. A cop! The cop with the pencil and note-book!

He was straining futilely at the ropes; trying to free himself. His neck was swollen and puffed. His face was purplish. His eyes were wide and staring. Harrigan choked with sardonic laughter. That was the why of the gag. They didn't want him to teach any tricks to the broken Arm of the Law.

His laughter ceased abruptly and his eyes narrowed in thought. Why was he still alive? Why were they taking precautions to keep him alive? The reason was obvious. They wanted something from him. The answer to some question; an idea of how much he knew; the names of other people who might be in the know. And Harrigan knew Frank Crocker's methods. Whatever the question was, they'd promise him freedom for his answer and, once that answer was given, a gun would roar and the name of Francis St. Xavier Harrigan would be added to the roll of New York's murder mysteries!

Harrigan bit savagely into the gag. They had him and they had him right. His only chance lay in keeping a tight mouth. And it mightn't be so easy!

Somewhere behind him, a key went into a lock. A door opened and shut again. Feet thumped on the floor. Into his range of vision came Frank Crocker—Ape Scalisi—Icky Yeager.

The three regarded the trussed-up policeman. Ape Scalisi, chewing tobacco, curved a brownish stream into the officer's purple face. Icky Yeager grinned. Frank Crocker said: "Save some. We got another customer over here." They turned to Harrigan.

Frank Crocker took a stand beside the couch. Icky Yeager sat down on the foot of it and took a pistol from his pocket. Ape Scalisi ripped off the gag. Frank Crocker said: "Now don't get foolish an' start lettin' out a yawp. That's what Icky's here for. You know what Icky can do with a gun."

Harrigan cleared his throat and told him exactly what he could do with it.

Frank Crocker sneered. "Still wise-crackin', eh? Well, we'll take care o' that, too." He stepped closer, bent forward a little and asked: "Where's the Kane account?"

Harrigan's heart bounded. They hadn't found the account. And that account was mighty important. If he could stall 'em, he might get a break. He asked: "What's the terms? What do I get if I tell?"

Frank Crocker's face was wooden. He said: "If you turn up that expense-account an' lay off till after election, I'll call it quits an' let you off."

Sincerity was in his voice; gravity was in his eyes; his entire demeanor was businesslike. It was a proposal that might have tempted a less experienced man, but Harrigan *knew*—knew that he knew too much to be freed; knew that, once he opened his mouth, he'd land on a Queensborough dump; knew that this was a game of Questions and Answers with blazing death as the stake. He asked: "What makes you so sure that I know where it is?"

Frank Crocker grimaced. "You stole it off my desk an' you didn't have a chance to pass it. It wasn't in the taxi an' it isn't on you now. I'm bein' big-hearted; givin' you a chance for your life. Where is it?"

A chance for his life! Harrigan's chuckle was grim as the death he expected. He said: "You sound like a Headquarters dick. All you need is the badge."

"Where's that account?"

"Getting ready for the paper, by this time."

"Ixnay. I had a man down there. They're not gettin' out an extra an' they don't know anythin'. You might as well come clean; run-arounds ain't stickin' today."

Harrigan smiled his sweetest. "Soon's we lost you for a few blocks. I slipped it into a stamped envelope I always carry, addressed to Roger Conwell, 'Personal—Important,' with a note to hold it until I showed up. Boy I tossed it to stuck it in a mail-box. Course they don't know anything at the office—yet."

Harrigan, watching intently, saw Yeager start and even Ape Scalisi frown. But Frank Crocker's eyes bored into his. Harrigan read their message. If it was true Crocker couldn't help himself; if it was a bluff, he'd call it.

"For the last time—what'd you do with that expense account?"

"If what I told you isn't true," said Harrigan, "then I ate it."

The politician's lips curved down. His voice had the edge of a razor-blade. "Not a bad idea," he said. "We'll have a look. Go get 'im, Wop!"

Ape Scalisi leaped forward. He bent over the reporter, ripped open vest and shirt, stripped underwear down with a sweep of a ham-like hand—laid Harrigan bare to the waist. He pulled out a queer-looking stubby pistol with a silencer on the barrel, clicked it open, slipped in a heavy, slug-less cartridge and looked at Frank Crocker.

The politician was looking at Harrigan. Eyes and voice were

level and cold. "It takes a long, long time to kill a man with blank cartridges—an' that's how I'm gonna have Scalisi kill you! He's gonna blast away till you talk; make a livin', breathin' hamburg outta you till you open up! You might as well know the truth: I'm gonna croak you anyway, but it's up to you how I do it. You can have your choice; spill your guts or let Scalisi spill 'em for you!" He turned to the Ape. "Get set, Wop. We'll start in the belly!"

Ape Scalisi muttered: "Suits me!" and jabbed Harrigan savagely in the wind. Harrigan gagged.

Frank Crocker closed the transom, pulled down the shade and switched on the light. He asked quietly: "Gonna talk?"

Harrigan set his teeth. He didn't know whether he could go through with the play or not. The odds were heavy against him but life is ever sweet. He didn't want to be found in a ditch. He gasped for breath; said: "Go to hell!"

Frank Crocker gestured to the Ape. The guerrilla prodded soft, white skin, selected a spot and pulled the trigger.

Harrigan lunged forward to meet the charge. Legs and arms strained at their ties. Stomach and chest went red with a sudden flush of color. His face was pale as death. His eyes were closed and crinkled. He gasped: "———!" and went slack in the ropes that held him.

Icky Yeager said: "Over the fence!" He holstered his gun in disgust and went out. Ape Scalisi raised shoe-button eyes from his victim and looked at Frank Crocker. Crocker snapped: "Bring 'im to! I'm gonna have that lousy sheet o' paper if I have to cut out his guts an' show 'em to him! Come on; hurry up!"

Scalisi went to the wash-stand and drew a pitcher of cold water. He came back to the cot and hurled it on Harrigan's face and chest. Harrigan stirred and made piteous sounds in his throat. Frank Crocker drew open the lower window slightly. The icy November wind did the rest.

Harrigan opened bloodshot eyes and stared through a film of agony. Ape Scalisi, grinning savagely, fondled the snub-nosed gun. Icky Yeager was not to be seen. Frank Crocker was asking, grimly: "Gonna come through?"

Memory stirred in Harrigan's pain-wracked brain. They were asking him a question. The answer to that question was his only claim to life. If he answered it, he'd die. Hell, he didn't want to die; not at thirty-four! Wordlessly, he shook his head.

Scalisi began to prime his gun. Crocker rapped: "All right, Wop; snap into it! We got no time for monkey-shines! Take an eye this time!"

Harrigan started and caught his lower lip between his teeth. Scalisi grinned from ear to ear; mouthed: "That hits 'im, Boss!" and raised the snub-nosed gun. He bent over Harrigan, hesitated a moment and said thoughtfully: "The left one looks the best. I'll fry that 'ne first!" The blood spurted as Harrigan's teeth sliced through his lip.

The door of the room burst open and Icky Yeager rushed in. He said quickly: "Kane's callin', Boss. The *Leader's* runnin' him ragged. The yellow's squirtin' out o' him. He won't get off the phone; you better talk to him!"

Frank Crocker whirled. "The damn' dummy!" he snarled viciously. "I've told him an' told him never get in touch with me! I'll talk to him, all right! I'll bring 'im up here an' slip 'im a dose o' this!" He sprang for the door; rasped over his shoulder: "Come on; we'll finish this after!" and ran for the stairs. Icky Yeager followed.

Ape Scalisi waddled his bow-legged bulk across the room, turned suddenly round and slapped his knee. "By ———! I knowed I was forgettin' somethin'!" He took deliberate aim and slung tobacco-juice at Harrigan.

Harrigan didn't even know it.

HARRIGAN BECAME AWARE that he was being shaken vigorously. It was nothing new; he had been roused so, several times. It was getting to be a game. He rolled his head to one side, said: "No!" thickly and relapsed into punch-drunk stupor.

The shaking continued. Harrigan opened weary eyes and gazed into the beefy face of the cop who was his cellmate. The cop put his finger to his lips; said softly: "Sssssh!"

Harrigan stared stupidly about. He put up a hand and rubbed his chin. His wrists and ankles ached. Realization came. He was free to move—untied! He cried: "What's—"

The cop laid a hand over Harrigan's mouth and hissed: "Shut up!" in a fierce whisper.

The reporter's eyes narrowed. The old think-tank began to boil. He brushed the officer's hand aside and sat up quickly. "To hell with noise," he said. "This is a sound-proof room." He clapped his hands to his middle, suddenly; gasped: "———! My stomach!"

The big policeman nodded sympathetically. "That was a hell of a thing they done to you, the ———! They was back since, tryin' to finish the job, but they couldn't bring you to, enough."

Harrigan reached for his handkerchief and said in the same breath! "Here, wet this," and: "How'd you get loose?"

The cop turned on the water in the wash-stand, soaked the

handkerchief and grunted: "Oh, I'm pretty strong. I just kept monkeyin' around. I knew I could do it if I got time enough." He handed the dripping cloth to the reporter and added: "An' besides, I kinda had that taxi-driver in my mind." He shivered a little. "That helped rush the job along."

Harrigan folded the sopping bit of rag and laid it tenderly over the angry red-black powder burn. His lips twisted in pain but he held the pad firmly in place, doubled his shirt over it and buttoned his vest tightly; asked: "What about the taxi-driver?"

"Oh—nothin'." The policeman was vague. "He woke up an' started to get tough. They—" He shrugged and drew his finger across his throat.

"Who?"

"The guy they call 'Wop,'" said the officer.

"Tough!" murmured Harrigan. "Now, how do we get out?"

"The cop made a puzzled gesture. "I thought you knew this layout. The door—"

"Not in a week," said Harrigan. "It's sound-proof. Heavier'n the anchors o' hell. How's the window?"

"Three-story drop." The policeman brightened suddenly. "You say this dump is sound-proof? We ain't gotta be careful o' noise? Hell; then it's easy!" He started looking around the room. "We can throw somethin' out an' attract attention. Then we can holler an' get a cop an'—"

Harrigan's eyes widened. "No, no!" he said. "That's out!"

The cop stared. "Whaddaya mean—out?" He hunted feverishly about the room.

Harrigan took an eager step forward and swore as clothing rubbed his wound. His voice was hoarse with excitement. "Listen! This'll make a whale of a story; I want to keep it exclusive. All I've got so far is a twenty-four-carat shellacking; I might as well get some credit, too. Take it easy for a second, while I figure it out."

The policeman paid no attention. "I'm gonna get out o' here," he said; "an' quick, too. You can figure all you want; me, I'm gettin' out!" He walked over to the iron cot; said: "I got a notion to toss this out." He hefted it; grinned. "That oughta bring a cop on the run!"

Harrigan's eyes glowed. The idea of scooping the town was taking firm hold on him. "Wait," he pleaded. "I'll think of a way to get out in a minute. This is Page One stuff for keeps and I want to make it a beat. If we land in a station-house, all the papers get it; don't you see?"

"The papers can have it," said the Law calmly. "I want no part of it! I woke you up 'cause I thought you might gimme some help an' all you've give me is arguments." He dragged the cot to the window and pulled up the shade; he asked: "Did you know there's four of 'em here now?"

"Four?"

"Yeah; Kane's come to join his flock."

"Kane? Ezra Kane! You sure?"

" 'Course I'm sure," grunted the cop. "Don't I know the politicians?" He started to raise the cot.

Harrigan bit his thumb-nails. His face lit up; he took a step forward and cried: "Wait! Wait! I've got a scheme!"

"Wait, hell!" snapped the officer. "I've got a wife an' kids!" He balanced the cot on one end and leaned forward to shove it over the sill. There was a flat report behind him. He threw up his hands, clawed at his throat, weaved uncertainly towards the window and crashed to the street below.

HARRIGAN, WHIRLING AT the faint scrape of the opening door, saw flame streak from Icky Yeager's gun and dived for the killer's weapon. Yeager cursed, lost his balance as Harrigan hit him and threw a wild shot. He staggered against the half-open door, heard a terrific noise on the stairs, steadied himself and fired—twice—into the blackness of the well.

Harrigan bounced off the killer's chest, gained the head of the stairs on hands and knees, saw a blacker shape in the blackness and knew that the stairs were blocked. His position was plainly untenable. Reinforcements would come from below; leaden messengers of death from above. There wasn't a moment to waste; Harrigan didn't. He launched himself headlong down the steps.

A man cried out in high-pitched alarm and tried—too late—to side-step. Harrigan hit him above the knees, threw him over his shoulder by momentum and went riding down the stairs on his chest with a wriggling, screaming burden across him.

Two flat reports came from above. Two thudding slaps came from behind. Then his face dug into a rough straw mat and his shoulders crashed the landing wall.

The man he'd hit on the stairs was all over him like a blanket. Harrigan spun on his back and grabbed him by the throat; the thin neck was limp in its stiff collar. Harrigan thought: "Knocked cold!" and fumbled over him for a weapon. His fingers touched something wet; something thick and sticky.

Harrigan's twisted smile flashed in the dark. He felt for the man's wrist. No pulse; no heart. Harrigan thought: "It's a damned good thing you were there, brother! That moqui shoots like Billy the Kid!"

His hands passed swiftly over the corpse. On the right hip

was a flat automatic. He drew it out, snapped off the catch, murmured: "Sweetheart!" and wriggled towards the lower stairs.

Something occurred to him suddenly. That high-pitched cry of fright—that high, stiff collar.... He bit his lip and reversed his direction; his fingers played over the body again. There was a sprinkling of hair around the ears and a cow-lick over the forehead. The top of the skull was smooth and bare; the nose was long and thin and bony. Harrigan gasped: "Ezra Kane, for a million! My ———! What a story!" A bullet plocked into the wall at his ear.

Harrigan groaned, hit the floor with his fist, threshed against the wall with his feet and lay still with his gun at the ready.

NO SOUND CAME from above. Heavy silence was everywhere. The darkness was thick as gravy. Everything seemed suddenly dead.

Outside could be heard faint cries. A police whistle raised dim echoes. An ambulance bell clanged on the wind. Harrigan thought: "My ———! I forgot! There's a copper dead; all Center Street'll be here soon!"

The reporter was in a hole. He had the reform racket all sewed up. He had to get out; hop a phone; make an edition. If he waited for the cops to raid, he'd lose a beautiful story; if he made a break, he was meat for Icky Yeager. Harrigan's lips tightened. This thing had gone too far; Kane's killing had settled it. The story was too big. If he muffed it now, he'd better give up reporting!

The landing walls were left and center; the stair-head must be to the right. He held the gun in his right hand, pushed himself up with his left. He came to his knees, then to his feet and edged slowly towards the stairs. On the landing above him, a board creaked.

Concealment was out of the question. He took the landing at a bound, hit the steps going down, heard bullets smack around him and came into the lower hall—straight as a homing pigeon. The front door was a light in the darkness. Through the glass, he had a glimpse of people gathering. Impossible to get out unnoticed!

He took a chance, swung to the left and ran down a dark hall with an arm stuck out before him. A door barred his way. He fumbled for a knob—found it—came into a sort of kitchenette.

Street-lights shone in through the windows, making his surroundings plain. At the other side of the room, a door swung free on its hinges. Beyond was a backyard—a high fence—glowing lights. Harrigan breathed: "Happy days!" bounded across the floor, hurled himself through the half-open door—straight into the arms of Ape Scalisi, just coming in.

Scalisi staggered from the sudden shock. He took a step back; then closed in, with a move surprisingly swift.

Harrigan's gun-hand was held high; the guerrilla raised it higher. He snapped a muscle-ridged arm around Harrigan's back; crushed him in deadly embrace.

Harrigan wrenched to one side to give the Ape the knee. Scalisi brought him closer; in at the waist, out at the shoulders—got set to break his back. Harrigan's breath was coming in gasps; his spine was beginning to Crack. Scalisi had gotten his bone-crushing hold. It would be a matter of seconds, now. No man could stand such pressure.

Scalisi exerted his giant strength. His bullet head dug into the reporter's chest. An ancient instinct roused in Harrigan's blood. He arched his neck, pulled back his head, bared his teeth and struck at one of Scalisi's flattened ears.

The guerrilla cried out like a beast in pain. His great muscles tensed spasmodically. He pulled Harrigan down and in with a convulsive movement. For the fraction of an instant, the muzzle of the gun rested under his armpit. In that instant Harrigan pressed the trigger twice. They hit the dirt together.

Harrigan got up; Scalisi didn't.

THE MANAGING EDITOR couldn't be found. The City Editor's kid was sick. Harrigan stamped in the drug-store phone booth. "My! What a sheet! Is it running itself?"

The head copy-boy's tone was upstage. "Mr. Conwell is in his office."

Old Roger Conwell—owner and publisher of the *Leader*—maker and breaker of politicians—latter-day Pulitzer! Harrigan's voice was almost a shout. "Plug me in on him; quick!"

Harrigan got him—just that way. He went into his story without a halt; rattled it off in headline style—phrases ready to slap into print. A beautiful bit of dictation.

The *Leader's* phones had four extensions. Two stenos took him word for word. Old Roger only interrupted once. He asked: "Where *is* that Kane expense account?"

Harrigan chuckled hoarsely. "That's where the laugh comes in! They didn't dare to bump me as long as I held it out. An' that's the kick-back, see. I don't know where the damn' thing went; I lost it in that taxi crash!" He was back in his word-spilling stride.

"Okey," he finished briefly. "That's all. Better send DeLavan to cover the raid. They'll be gettin' Yeager; Crocker's gone. I'll be at the nearest hospital. My belly hurts like hell."

Old Roger snapped: "Hold everything!"

A momentary silence; then: "Ezra Kane is dead in the same apartment that the policeman and Scalisi died in?"

"Yeah."

"No weapons on or about Kane's person?"

"No; not now."

"Nothing to indicate that Kane and the officer of the law were not tricked there and brutally murdered?"

"Well—no."

"Fine!" Old Roger's voice grew fainter. He was speaking to someone beside him. "That's the way the story'll go: *'Reformer Murdered by Racketeers.'*"

Harrigan cried: "Hello! Hello! That's the lead every sheet in town'll carry! Hell, man! I'm giving you the inside stuff!"

"It's no good!" Old Roger's voice carried excitement. Again he was speaking beside the phone. "Rip the forms! Page One and Editorial! I'll supervise the layout, personally!"

Then: "Hello, Harrigan! This is under your hat, see! This killing on the eve of election will swing voting opinion into a reform landslide! That reform ticket's a good one! Kane was the only blotch and he's gone! The city needs the rest of those men. We'll hold off with the Crocker connection and give New York a reform administration. It's all for the best, my boy!"

"But—"

"Go butt your head! I'm still running this paper, Harrigan! And, listen; don't you get the kick in it? That ticket was practically constructed by Crocker's racketeers to give Ezra Kane a chance of election. Now, Kane's killing will elect the rest of 'em! There's a *real* kick-back for you, my boy! It's beautiful! Can't you see it?"

Harrigan's voice was very dry. "Yeah," he said. "I'm laughing!"

THE DOCTOR WAS heavy-eyed and sleepy. He said wearily: "Well, what is it now?"

Harrigan winced and unbuttoned his shirt.

Sleepiness fled from the medico. He stared wide-eyed; his tone was shocked.

"My ————! man! What've you been up to?"

Harrigan's lips twisted. The crooked grin distorted his face. He said: "I was monkeyin' with a kick-back, Doc. An' the damn' thing did!"

Dead Evidence

Harrigan, the "leaded ink" specialist,
gets pulled into a hard, tight jam

HARRIGAN CAME IN like a blast of the cold November wind. His mouth was sullen, his dark brows low over smoldering eyes. He whirled through the *Leader's* City-Room, slammed the Managing Editor's door, banged into a straight-backed chair. "How's for my dough? I'm through!"

The Managing Editor's eyes were quizzical. "What's the matter, now? Row with Old Roger again?"

"Old Roger, be damned! We settled up this afternoon."

The M.E. grinned. "You're telling me? Everybody in the block listened in. Every City-Room in town knows it. The operator was gonna call a cop. She thought you were murdering each other."

Harrigan rasped; "It *is* murder!"

The M.E. said: "Not as bad as that. I'll admit it's a shame to kill a good story, but—it isn't murder."

Harrigan leaned forward, snap-brim hat on the back of his head. "The hell it isn't! When you pin a killing on a guy that's a political power in this town—a guy that's known an' respected—a little tin god! When you show him up as a racketeer—a coldblooded murderer! An' then have your owner kill the story for reasons of 'political expediency!' The hell it ain't murder!"

The Managing Editor's eyes narrowed. He said: "I wasn't in on the story. Nobody was. But I knew it had something to do with the Kane killing—" He asked queerly: "Who's the 'political power?'"

Harrigan said thickly: "Frank Crocker! He owns Icky Yeager. An' Yeager rubbed Kane!"

The M.E. tensed, leaned suddenly forward, sniffed the air suspiciously. "You're drunk, Harrigan!"

Harrigan's anger flared again. "An' why'n hell wouldn't I be drunk! I find a guy in Mike's that buys me drinks; it's the only break I get since I worked on this lousy rag. All I hear is 'politics'—'political expediency.' Old Conwell wants the reform-ticket in. But Crocker had a finger in it. An' if Crocker's exposed as a killer, the publicity'll be bad for the ticket!"

Harrigan's voice was getting thicker. "———— ————! for the sake of a lousy bit o' politics, Ol' Conwell 'll have the town a walkin' shootin' gallery! Crocker bosses Icky Yeager—the shootin'est hood in the city—an' nobody's wise. An' Conwell kills my story—the best ———— damn' story I ever put my name to!"

The M.E. leaned forward, took him by the lapels of his rough tweed coat. "Easy," he said. "Take it easy. The whole City-Room 'll be listenin' in." He regarded his star reporter sourly. "A hell of a fine specimen, you are, to be squawkin' civic righteousness. All's the matter with you—you're stinkin' drunk an' you've had a story held up on you. Your vanity's aching. Get the hell outta here an' sober up. You're a good man an' Conwell 'll probably overlook the trouble you're makin'."

Harrigan jerked himself free. "To hell with you—an' to hell with Conwell! Gimme my dough!" He fumbled by his side, looked down, burst out: "Well, by ———! I even lost my cane! If I ain't gettin' breaks!"

The M.E. growled: "You'll get a break in your skull if you don't—" He reached for the ringing phone; said: "Hello; oh, yes, Mr. Conwell; right here." He covered the transmitter with his hand. "Hey, you. Straighten up. The Old Man wants to talk to you."

Harrigan's head snapped up. Conwell's name in his ears was like smoke in the nose of an old fire-horse. He grabbed the phone, barked: "Harrigan speaking. What is it?" Then the sullen mouth straightened, the lips thinned. "What the hell for? There's nothin' to be said. I said it all this afternoon."

He leaned across the desk. The front of his tweed overcoat caught on the corner. Light struck the Colt .45 in his armpit. "What's that? Listen—there's no use.... I'll only get mad, again.... Oh, all right!"

He slammed down the receiver, got uncertainly to his feet. "Conwell wants to see me. Wants me to come to the house. More chin about this Frank Crocker-Icky Yeager murder combination. Why'n hell don't Conwell leave me alone; leave me quit—before he gets his nose punched!"

The M.E. said: "You hadn't ought to run around soused—packin' a gun."

Harrigan rasped: "You hadn't oughta be so ——— damn' free with your advice!"

The slamming door jerked at its hinges.

"OLD ROGER" CONWELL, owner and publisher of the *Leader*, lived in the Mauve Decade. His manners and morals and mode of life were governed by Eighteen-Ninety. He lived now, as he had then, with half-blind Hawkins to "do" for him.

His house off the Avenue had once been a show-place. Now it was a show-place again—a relic of bygone times. The only concession was a built-in, street-level garage. And the automobile that it housed was stolen twice a month. Old Roger had never locked up a horse; why should he lock up a car?

Harrigan stumbled out of the taxi; surveyed the gloomy pile.

On the opposite sidewalk, a man swung briskly away. A tall, slim man in a rough tweed coat. Harrigan focused wavering eyes, stiffened suddenly; breathed: "Icky—"

Then the cold wind whipped his face; he laughed shakily, muttered: "That damn' booze!" and climbed the wooden stairs.

He rang the bell, listened to its strident echo; waited in the dimly-lit porte-cochère. No one came to answer.

Harrigan grew impatient. What the hell, he'd been asked to come. He rang the bell again; muttered: "Ol' Hawkins must be deaf as well 's blind," and gave the heavy door a kick. It swung inward without a sound.

Harrigan watched it click to behind him, said: "Wish to hell I'd kicked a bank!" and surveyed the empty hall. Old Roger's coat hung on a rack; in the stand beside it, was a cane.

There was something familiar about that cane. Harrigan stepped forward, leaned close to the head, focused erratic eyesight. There could be no doubt; the cane was his own.

He straightened up; grinned at the hat-rack; "I do tricks with doors; I find things I lost; by ———! I'm gonna stay drunk forever!"

He turned, staggered a little and ascended the stairs.

Light showed above the banisters; light from Old Roger's library. Harrigan knocked, heard no answer, opened the door—and was suddenly sober. The body of Roger Conwell was sprawled across a chair.

Harrigan gagged and breathed deeply; the liquor went out with a breath-taking rush. He threw off weakness—took a brace—stepped close to the dead man.

His foot struck something that rolled from under it; something that glittered in the light. He stooped—picked up an ejected cartridge—caliber .45. He muttered: "Coincidence," tossed it on the desk; fumbled for Conwell's wrist.

Old Roger was still warm; blood welled slowly from his breast. A high-powered bullet—fired close—had bitten a hole in his heart. In at the front, out at the back—clean as Man-o'-War's heels. Harrigan gasped: "The guy in the street!" whirled and leaped for the stairs. From a door in the hall, came muffled noise.

Harrigan paused in half-stride; his gun snapped into his hand. He rapped: "Who's there?" and approached the door. The dull sound came again.

Light streamed out from the murder-room but the side of the hall was in shadow. Harrigan stepped to the side of the door; leaned from behind the jamb. He turned the knob with his left hand, the gun held low in his right.

The door opened under his push; light shone on tied-up ankles. Harrigan grasped them—pulled hard; drew Hawkins into the hall. Hawkins—bound and gagged!

Harrigan bent swiftly—whipped the gag from the butler's mouth. His voice was sharp, high-pitched: "Quick! Quick! Who was it? Tell me!"

The butler drew breath in a shuddering sigh and worked his cramped jaw-muscles. Pain contorted his wrinkled features. He mumbled: "Oh, my head!"

Harrigan prodded him: "Come, come! Who's been in here tonight?"

The old man's rheumy eyes grew sharp; spots of color seeped into his cheeks; sudden indignation strengthened his voice. "And what, Mr. Harrigan, is the meaning of this, may I ask?"

Harrigan snapped: "Never mind questions. Conwell's been shot; murdered! What do you know—hurry up!"

Hawkins' jowls sagged grayly. His mouth hung open. He gasped: "Murdered! You—"

Harrigan's fingers worked in and out. His liquor-edged nerves were trying to scream. His voice was hoarse and jerky. "For the love o'——— come out of it! What happened? Who came in?"

Creases appeared in the butler's forehead; fright came into his goggling eyes. "No one but you—all evening!" His tones were suddenly shrill. "Murderer! The whiskey is still on your breath! You've kil—"

Harrigan shook him silent. His voice was low and hard. "For ——— sake, shut up! What're you talking about! Now—an' make it snappy!—who was the other guy?"

The butler's face was pale; his nearsighted eyes protruded.

But his voice came, surprisingly strong: "You can't trick me so simply, Harrigan. I'm old but I'm not a fool! A change of voice won't— Stop! Oh! You're breaking my arm!"

Harrigan's fingers relaxed their grip; he steadied himself with an effort, said hoarsely: "When'd I change my voice? What made you think it was me?"

The cunning of desperation gleamed in Hawkins' eyes. His voice shook but the words held. "I knew you. Your hat—your coat—your cane. And the odor of liquor was strong—"

"When was this? When, man?"

Hawkins' eyes held insane light. Fear was getting the upper hand; the shaky voice was cracking. "When you came. When I asked you to leave. When you struck me with a pistol—"

Hysteria conquered the aged servant; the house rang to his half-crazed shriek. "Murderer! Murderer! Kill me, too; go on—kill me!"

A picture was searing Harrigan's brain; the little green door at Sing Sing! People knew he had come to see Conwell—come to see him drunk and armed. Old Roger had stopped a .45. Hawkins' story would get him the chair—

The butler's life hung on a thread as Harrigan's creaking nerves gave way. His gun bore down sharply; his face was a snarling mask. "A frame, eh! A murder-trap! I'll see you in hell—" he paused abruptly.

Downstairs, were running feet. Clubs rattled the outer door. A voice—the voice of authority—spoke: "Come on; open up! Police!"

Harrigan growled like a baited bear and whirled to the head of the stairs. He went half-way down in a headlong plunge, vaulted the banister into the hall—heard Hawkins' "Murder!"

shrill through the house—and raced for the rear of the building.

Behind him, revolver-butts splintered glass; the parlor echoed to pounding feet.

He spun through a door at the end of the hall—came into the darkened kitchen. At the further end was gleaming light—a door with a frosted window. He bounded towards it, reached for the knob—slid to a jarring halt.

A visored cap was dark on the glass; a club was rising to smash it!

HARRIGAN'S HEART HIT sledgehammer blows; his breath rasped in his throat. He was framed like a picture on the wall; the flame-chair's arms were reaching— Then his whirling brain clicked into high; he went hurtling across the kitchen.

The garage was flush with the sidewalk; hooked on to the side of the house. He bumped into chairs, caromed off tables, felt swinging doors give before him and went to his knees in a serving-hall.

From the front of the house, came shouts of: "Stop!" Back in the kitchen were scudding feet. A gun roared; a bullet shattered crockery. Harrigan raced along the hall. That damned door must be somewhere—

His elbows rattled panels. He grasped a knob, spun a key in a lock; the door did not open. In back of him, the swing-door banged—grunting humans hit the hall.

Harrigan snarled and wrenched at the door; a bullet bit into the wall beside him. Then his desperate fingers made a spring-lock, threw the catch, jerked open the door. He leaped through, slammed it behind him, missed a step, whirled heels-over-head down a short flight of stairs, brought up with a jerk in Old Roger's garage.

Street-lights shone through high-set windows; gleamed on the dark-blue Cadillac.

Harrigan knew Old Roger's habits; hoped he hadn't changed. He scrambled to his feet, flung open the door of the car; his reaching hand struck dangling keys.

In the hall above, were running feet. A weight thudded the hall door. The groaning panels sagged and gave. A hoarse voice was sharp with surprise: "There's the ————! Let 'im have it!"

Guns roared at close quarters; a side window shivered to bits. Harrigan's hat jerked on his head; upholstery sheared apart beside him. Then the big Cadillac snarled into speed, smashed through the doors with rending sound and surged across the sidewalk.

Harrigan, low across the wheel, swung to the left sharply. The great car staggered, held its own, straightened into a crosstown run. Police-whistles made shrill echo.

Harrigan gave her all she had, took a reckless right-hand turn. He slowed abruptly, veered to the left, kissed the Caddy good-bye in the next block. In an East Side express, he thought it over.

His lips grew thin and his gray eyes bleak as he visualized the murder-trap. The trap had been built by a master-framer— even to Hawkins' damning story. There was little to be done; he was due to fry, to burn for the Conwell kill. Everything stacked against him; except—

He muttered grimly: "No use excepting; a chance in a thousand—at best!"

AT LEADER SQUARE, he climbed to the side-walk; looked up at the *Leader's* lights. Many a front-page spread he'd given 'em—sensational stories by the score, but never the equal of this! He muttered with sardonic humor: "Star Reporter Hits New High!" and headed for his favorite speakie.

Mike was alone in his place. He catered to newspaper men and the hawks were making editions. He looked up, surprise on his beefy face. "Well, lookit what's here! The original human tank!"

Harrigan said: "H'lo, Mike. A whiskey-sour. Whatsa matter with you?"

"Matter?" The bartender made wide eyes. "You should ask! After that load you took outta here, while ago!"

Harrigan grinned; said: "What th' hell; didn't cost me anything."

Mike shoved a glass across the bar; laughed. "Yeah; that's so. Whatta you got on that guy, anyway? A murder-rap?"

Harrigan almost held his breath; grunted: "Who?"

The bartender frowned. "Who? Why, Vergez, o' course. The guy that was pourin' 'em inter you."

"Oh, him," Harrigan sighed. "Just happened I done him a favor."

"Well"—Mike reached for the rag—"it musta been a good one. I'm tendin' here fer five years an' I never see him buy a drink before. Gen'ly he's tryin' ta bum the price o' one." He grinned, picked up the empty glass. "If I'd ever saw a reporter with money, I'd thought he was fixin' ta roll you."

Harrigan shrugged. "What'd he want to roll me for? Had plenty dough, didn't he?"

The barman polished the glass; brought out the bottle.

"Seemed to," he admitted. "An' shootin' off about more to come, tonight." He measured the shot with expert eye. "But I don't go for that. An' if I was you, I'd lay off them steerers; them punks like Vergez—they ain't nothin' but trouble in 'em."

Harrigan said: " 'S the way I figure. This Vergez ain't on my callin' list; it just happened I give him a hand. I don't even know the guy; who he is, or anythin'."

"He's cheap stuff." Mike put the whiskey-sour on the bar. "A no-good punk. I figured maybe you wasn't hep to 'im. Slugger at th' polls, look-out on loft jobs—stuff like that. Anythin' fer a buck. One o' them rats in Deegan's flop. Shouldn't be allowed in a white man's bar." He shrugged; said resignedly: "These times, you gotta stand fer it."

The second whiskey stopped half-way to Harrigan's lips. He whirled; said over his shoulder: "Jeeze; I gotta meet a man!" and banged the door behind him.

Mike grinned at the untasted glass. He thought: "Hope you don't meet 'im on my clean steps!"

"DEEGAN'S" WAS A ramshackle, three-story structure. Its outer appearance belied its interior. Dark streets bounded it; cracked flagging surrounded it; a stone's-throw away, were the docks.

The first two floors were thickly curtained; the third was the flop for Deegan's rats. An outside staircase yawned invitation; those that accepted were weary of life.

Harrigan mounted, gun in hand. From the lower floors came subdued sound; his cat-footed tread was completely muffled.

He gained the swaying landing, opened a creaking door, came into a nauseous, unlit hall.

Twin streaks of light from under doors marked two wakeful roomers. One was close to him on the left; the other, far down the hall to the right. Harrigan's hard eyes narrowed. The census of rats was slim—but it might be hard to take.

He stepped quickly across to the first gleam of light, bumped the door with his shoulder. A heavy voice came through the panels: "Who's it? Whaddaya want?"

Harrigan thought: "Wrong number," and staggered noisily. The heavy voice said: "Damn' lush!"

Harrigan muttered: "Neighborly guys!" and went swiftly along the hall. The other light came from the end room; a cubicle stuck against the wall.

Harrigan tapped on the panels guardedly; heard a shuffle of feet inside. Then a reedy voice came through the door: "Who's there?"

Harrigan stiffened at the sound; his pulses came leaping up. He leaned close to the door, his shoulder low; said in muffled tones: "All right, Vergez. Th' dough."

A key creaked in a lock; the door opened half a foot. A dark, squatty man peered out. He said: "All right," let the door go slack, stepped back into the room. Then his close-set eyes went suddenly wide and the reedy voice climbed upward. "Hey! You're—" The heavy Colt dented his ribs. He gasped and mouthed curses.

Harrigan said with grim humor: "These overcoats are foolin' everybody." His eyes swept over the room.

The lay-out was dingy past compare. Sagging cot, rickety chair, a three-legged dresser—a dirty curtain across a corner. The iron rungs of a fire-escape grilled the single window.

Harrigan locked the door left-handed, crossed the room with leveled gun. He raised the dirty curtain, saw nails driven into the wall supporting nondescript garments, let it drop again. He rapped: "Come on; let's have it! Who'd you think I was?"

Vergez was standing beside the cot. His olive-skinned face was very pale. His lips drew back from pointed teeth. He snarled: "You'll find out, wiseguy!"

Harrigan had no time to waste; he rounded the bed swiftly. His jaw was set in lumpy lines; his eyes glittered under heavy brows. He said: "I will!" in brittle tones. "I will find out, you ———!"

Vergez retreated in quick alarm, threw out an arm, opened his mouth. "Hel—"

Harrigan's left cut off his wind. A swishing gun-barrel broke his nose. He gagged thickly, his eyes bulged; his tongue protruded between his teeth.

Then the strangling pressure on his throat relaxed and words grated through him like files on steel.

"Talk, damn you; talk! Talk or I'll kill you! Who put up the price of getting me drunk? Who paid you to steal my cane? Who's the pay-off; when's he coming?"

Vergez whimpered like a child in pain; his hand sought his shattered nose. Harrigan jerked it away, right arm raised in threatening gesture. "Who's the pay-off? Quick!"

Vergez moaned: "Icky Yeager," and sank, half-fainting to the bed.

Harrigan's gray eyes held cold light; his thin lips twitched in a crooked grin. He said: "My friend—Icky Yeager!" He shook the recumbent form; asked roughly: "When's he coming?"

Vergez's hand cradled his nose; his palm was full of blood. His muffled words blew crimson bubbles. "I dunno; after midnight."

Harrigan said: "It's after midnight, now; must be after one." His eyes slanted to the crimson face. He asked curiously: "What're you gettin'? What's the price o' fillin' me full o' Mike's whiskey?"

Vergez's voice was half a sob. "A lousy yard! An' I wish to ———— I'd never heard o' you!"

The crooked smile flashed on Harrigan's face. "A lotta people'll wish that!" He frowned, thumb-nail sawing his dark mustache; muttered very low: "They wouldn't dare hold out. This guy might figure the play an' let out an awful holler. Icky'll come, all right; he'll pay."

He picked up the rickety chair, growled: "Yeah; he'll pay!" and shoved it through the curtain. He said aloud: "Hey, you; I'm waitin' for your boyfriend, see. When he comes, you let him in. An' let him in with the glad hand. Put on the act; an' make it good—or there won't be any encores." He sat down on the chair, dangled the Colt by its trigger-guard—handy for Icky Yeager.

After a time, Vergez sat up; swabbed at his face with the bedding. Harrigan looked at him, almost with pity; thought: "You certainly earned that C—" And went taut at a tap on the window.

Vergez turned; his eyes grew wide—flickered obliquely to Harrigan's gun. He rose slowly, white of face, stood staring towards the window. The tapping came again.

Inch by inch, without a sound, Harrigan rose from the chair. He was watching Vergez like a hawk, the .45 straight before him. He couldn't see the window—the dirty curtain cut off his view; but his eyes bored into the grease-ball.

Vergez was like a man in a trance. He started forward with

dragging steps, staring straight at the window. Three slow steps under Harrigan's gun; then the curtain hid him from view. Harrigan swore a silent oath, heard the window go up with protesting creak, grasped at the edge of the curtain.

Vergez's hoarse voice whispered: "Listen," wound up in a shriek; a dull thud rattled the window. Then Harrigan leaped through the curtain, cursing himself for a fool.

Vergez lay half-way across the sill, his body blocking the window. Harrigan reached him at a bound, dragged him backward into the room—averted his eyes from a sickening sight. Vergez's skull had been crushed by a blow.

On the fire-escape was the click of heels; Harrigan dived head-first through the window.

A dark form was zig-zagging down the swaying escape— passing a window on the second floor. Harrigan caught the flashing picture— Slim man in a tweed coat; hawk face under snap-brim hat. Then his weight was on the steel-barred landing and the Colt jerked in his hand.

The bullet screamed from a steel rung. The man below looked up startled—redoubled his downward speed. Harrigan snarled at the bullet-proof ladders; went plunging down, four steps at a time.

Excited voices cried out from the curtained lower floors. Windows flung up on the fire-escape banged hastily down as armed men sprang past.

Harrigan gained at every leap. The slugger hit ground a scant flight in advance. He whirled in the shelter of the weighted drop, raced to the end of the building-wall and spun the corner at top speed.

Harrigan clamped the gun in his teeth, vaulted a dozen feet

into space—hit the sidewalk in full stride. In the street beyond, an engine roared.

Harrigan strained like Zev in the stretch. He was hot on the scent of the murder-trap. Yeager *mustn't* get away!

His flying feet spurned the cement; his hunched shoulders split the air. As he rounded the corner, he knew he was wrong.

A descending arm was blurred in motion; the lethal slung-shot a foot away. He remembered thinking of Vergez's head as the world blew up around him.

HARRIGAN AWOKE TO the sound of cymbals; wished to God the clangor would stop. He looked around him with cloudy eyes, saw a windowless basement room—knew that the cymbals were in his head.

He lay on his spine in a sway-backed chair, the posture was most uncomfortable. He put his hands on the arms of the chair, pulled himself slowly up. His eyes came more on a level and widened in swift surprise. The answers to all his troubles were staring him in the face.

Across the room from him, two men sat, one at each end of a table. One was tall, slim and hawk-faced with rough tweed coat and snap-brim hat. In poor light, he might have been Harrigan.

The other was shorter and heavily built. He had wide-set, level eyes and a stone-crusher jaw. His jet-black hair held the slightest of waves—was thick as a lion's mane.

Harrigan said through cracked, dry lips: "In this corner, Frank Crocker; his able second, Icky Yeager!"

Yeager sneered: "Just a wise-crackin' yap." He took a gun from his pocket and balanced it carefully in his hand.

Crocker raised an arm in majestic gesture. Yeager growled and lowered the gun.

Harrigan said in a weary tone: "Let's skip the preliminaries. Let 'im blast an' have it over."

Frank Crocker chuckled in high, good humor: "No, no; nothing like that. Icky wanted to but it isn't necessary. We'll have no killing here."

Harrigan blinked his eyes. "You mean—"

Crocker's smile was saccharine. "Don't you remember?" he asked. "You busted in here, roarin' drunk. Waving a gun in my face; hollering something about Roger Conwell being murdered. I tried to get you to go quietly, but you got careless with the rod. I hadda tap you on the head to keep you from hurting yourself."

He picked a gun from the table before him, held it carefully by the barrel; said in judicial tones: "There's a shell missing. Maybe you hurt somebody before you got here."

Harrigan said: "Too bad; I missed."

Crocker turned his head, grinned at the lowering gunman. "Can you imagine! He doesn't get it!"

Yeager sneered: "You dummy; that's the gun that killed Conwell!"

Crocker murmured: "I'm afraid it is. As a law-abiding citizen, I shall have to call the police."

Harrigan, knuckles white on the arms of the chair, muttered: "Frank Crocker—Master-Framer!"

Crocker bowed ironically. "Thanks. But a great deal of the credit goes to you. By ramming head-on into us, you've just about cinched yourself. If you'd slowed up and let yourself get arrested, you might've established reasonable doubt."

Harrigan passed fingertips across his aching head. He said: "Yeah? I don't see it."

Crocker's plump, manicured hand made an expansive sweep. "Oh, there were loop-holes," he said. "The murder-bullet wouldn't correspond with a bullet fired from your gun. And the time-element would practically preclude the possibility of your having left the house to ditch the murder-gun. Then there's Hawkins, who put the finger on you, according to the extras." He grinned. "Hawkins is more than half-blind; his testimony could be shot full o' holes."

Harrigan grimaced; said: "Lousy!"

Crocker stroked his heavy mane. "That isn't all," he said. "There's the cane. That was an error. Anything so personal would be bound to be missed. And, once you missed it, you'd probably mention the fact to a dozen people who'd testify that you didn't have it with you and couldn't have left it at Conwell's house." He smiled satisfaction. "Not that those things would clear you but they'd go far towards establishing reasonable doubt of your guilt."

Under heavy brows, Harrigan's eyes were sudden fire. He said in a voice that was far away: "I get it! I get it, now!"

Frank Crocker murmured softly: "Just a bit too late, I'm afraid."

Harrigan said: "Maybe." He threw a sidelong glance at Yeager. "Still—it wouldn't be so good if Headquarters busted in. You—with the gun. Yeager—dressed like me. My story'd have a chance of sticking."

Yeager looked up quickly; started to speak a piece.

Frank Crocker laughed assurance. "Don't worry," he said. "The police won't break in. They'll be invited. And Icky won't be here when they come. And, don't forget, I took this gun—the murder-gun—away from you."

His hand passed over his hair in smoothing gesture. "The only time I was nervous in this little deal was when Conwell was calling you with Icky's gun in his ear. I thought he might tip you off some way." He laughed again. "But you were so plastered, you wouldn't have noticed anyway."

Harrigan frowned; said: "But I don't get the Headquarters angle. Why bother with the police when—"

Crocker stood up, rubbed pudgy palms together. "I'm doing my simple duty; my duty as a good citizen. I'm thinking of going into business and it'll be good publicity." He pointed his finger at Harrigan, spoke in a schoolmaster tone: "Besides, don't you see, it'll give you a motive for any squawk you might want to make about me. I turn you up. All right—you try to get even by peddling fantastic yarns about me. Nobody'll give you a rumble." His laughter rolled again.

Yeager rasped: "To hell with th' cops! Le'me bump this punk! If he's dead, he can't holler—"

Crocker's tones were suddenly cold. "You'll do as I damned well tell you!" He turned. "I'm going upstairs to put in a Headquarters call. When I come back, you take the air. I'll stay with our guest and explain matters to the flyin' squad."

He slid the murder-gun in his pocket; said: "This is a very important toy," and opened the door to the house above. Long carpeted stairs showed through the opening.

HARRIGAN WATCHED THE door close, heard Crocker's soft tread recede on the carpet; said in musing tones: "If Crocker were out of the way, we could deal."

Yeager's eyes widened.

Harrigan looked at him quickly; asked: "Don't you get this, at all? Crocker's got cold feet. He's quittin'; through with the racket for keeps."

The gunman rasped: "So what?"

Harrigan said quickly: "He made his big play for political control of New York. He flopped an' the flop's got him shaky. He's got nice profits. All right—he takes 'em an' drags to hell out."

Yeager balanced the gun in his hand; said roughly: "Stow th' gab! Wot's it to you anyway? You won't know nothin' about it!"

Harrigan smiled tightly; said in a hard voice: "An' damned little *you'll* know about it!"

Icky's dark brows drew down. "Wot th' hell—"

Amazement was plain on Harrigan's face. "An' you're dope enough to think Crocker'll screw out an' leave you layin' around loose?"

The torpedo glanced towards the closed door. A wolfish smile spread on his somber face. "Don't you worry none about me, guy. Crocker's got plenty. When he quits, his high gun is keepin' him lots o' company."

Harrigan shook his head; muttered: "————! You're dumb!"

Yeager's beady eyes glinted. He rasped: "Go easy, guy; or them cops'll get cold meat, yet!" His hand moved.

Harrigan leaned forward slightly; said: "Listen, nitwit. Was Crocker ever tied in with a kill? Wasn't he always in the clear? The master mind that gave the orders? Sure; till he played for political control an' got messed in the Kane kill!"

Harrigan's low words came faster and faster. "Listen; there were three of us had dope on that; on the Kane kill. You an' me an' Roger Conwell. Conwell's gone an' I'm going! Why? Because Crocker's covering up!"

The torpedo's mouth was framing words. Harrigan's low voice beat him to it. "He even ordered Vergez rubbed—a guy that didn't know a ———— damn! It was just a chance he might get spoutin' to some good head."

Harrigan broke off with dramatic gesture; laughed shortly: "An' *you*—with all *you* know about Crocker! Where th' hell do you think *you're* coming off?"

The gunman shifted in his chair; his beady eyes were points of light. He muttered: "Crocker wouldn't…. He ain't got th' guts…." His harsh laugh was uncertain. "What th' hell're you givin' me, guy!"

Harrigan rapped: "I'm givin' you a chance for your lousy life—if you've got the brains to grab it!" He looked at the watch on his wrist; it was broken. He said: "H.Q. calls're handled fast. Crocker's been gone six minutes; long enough to call Montreal. Hell! He's not callin' anybody; he's just waitin' for the shot!"

Yeager rasped: "What shot?"

"The shot that'll tell him I'm dead! Don't you get it, you sap! That's why he left us alone. That's why he took the murder-gun. He figures I'll take a chance on jumpin' you. You'll cut me down. He'll come runnin' in with the gun in his hand—ask you what's the matter. He'll be close before you know—feed you a quick slug—drop the gun on the floor an' lam! Everything'll be cleared up. You an' I'll have shot it out; the cops'll have a finished case."

Harrigan's voice raised a trifle; threw the snapper quick. "What th' hell d'you think he took th' Conwell gun for? So he can leave it here to pin that kill on us!"

Yeager was half-way up in his chair. His face was working; his voice was hoarse. "By ———! If I thought—"

Harrigan's quick ears caught sound on the stairs. He scuffled his feet noisily; rapped: "Try it! Burn off a shot! You'll see!"

Yeager drew breath sharply. "If you're—"

Harrigan leaned far forward; made scraping noise with the chair-legs. His voice was low and hard; his eyes were molten steel.

"If you got the guts—try it!"

Yeager pivoted for a swing. The steady gun-barrel moved an inch. The walls recoiled from crashing sound.

Running feet were plain on the stairs. The door flung wide to frame Frank Crocker—jaw out-thrust, gun in his right hand, half raised. And his first glance was not for the prisoner, but was turned to Icky Yeager.

"You ——— ———!" he snarled. "Now——— ———"

Icky Yeager's chair went whirling backwards. His body was crouched; his swarthy face was almost black. He gritted: "You double-crossin'———"

Crocker read murder in the burning eyes, acted on sheer instinct. He leaped aside, jerked up the Conwell gun, threw a hurried shot at his hawk-faced torpedo.

The gun in Yeager's hand spat flame. Crocker jack-knifed from the knees, took the second slug in his heavy throat, then Harrigan leaped for the killer's gun-wrist.

The gunman caught the fleeting shadow; whirled with trigger half-way back. Harrigan's hand was a split second faster; the bullet made breath on his cheek.

Curses boiled in Yeager's throat; quick movement rippled his muscles. He flung half-way round, spun quickly back, struck for the eyes with a claw-fingered left.

Harrigan ducked, jerked the gunman forward; came up almost behind him. His reaching arms passed through Yeager's armpits; his left hand fastened on Yeager's neck.

The torpedo's head came snapping down; his high left hand clawed empty air; he figured a desperate play. He heaved to the right, threw his weight on the pinioned gun-wrist, jerked the gun in an inside swing.

Harrigan's right was sudden steel. The gun, pointing inward, stabbed Yeager's middle. Terrific pressure bent the cords in his wrist, tugged at the crooked trigger-finger.

A scream strangled in Yeager's throat. Words came in gasping breath. "Let up! Quick! Crocker's dead; we'll deal!…"

Sweat streamed from Harrigan's face. He said from deep in his chest: "I play 'em—like you do, Icky. Dead evidence—doesn't argue!" Supreme exertion crimsoned his temples. The gun—muffled in clothing—boomed dully.

Yeager's head went slack; his eyes glazed in their sockets. He panted: "Double-crossin'———! Framed Crocker—framed me!" Blood bubbled in his throat. "You worked it—to get in the clear—" The blood came with a rush.

Harrigan gasped breath into spent lungs, fumbled with Yeager's overcoat. From an inner pocket, he drew the hard object—his own gun. He was turning the corner, a block away, when the squad-car screamed to the curb.

HARRIGAN CROUCHED ON the fire- escape, raised the window an inch, waited for the hall to clear. His big chance was beckoning now. Crocker would never have cracked; neither would Yeager—but this was a different matter.

People moved back and forth in the hall. The *Leader* Building hummed with activity. Never had the sheet drawn such a night. A reporter and a sob-sister traversed the corridor—a reporter—another reporter; then Harrigan was in like a flash, took six long steps and ripped open the door of Managing Editor Carney's office.

Carney was dictating; his stenographer faced the door. She looked up, saw the tall, grim-faced figure before her and went rigid against the back of the chair. Her cheeks blanched, her mouth opened; she said something that sounded like: "E-e-e-k!"

Carney frowned at her, swiveled around in his chair. His dictation halted in mid-word; his eyes grew wide and wider; he choked: "Har—Harri—"; pulled himself together and spoke in a voice that was meant to be harsh: "Why are you here—and how? There are detectives on guard at the entrance." His hand crept towards a button on the desk.

Harrigan said quickly: "Go ahead; push it. They don't want me—not now."

Carney's hand hesitated. His gaze was fixed—staring. "What— They don't—"

"Not now." There was finality in Harrigan's tones. "Not since they pulled Crocker an' Yeager."

"Pulled—!" It ended in a gasp. Fear was white in Carney's face.

"Yeah. Half hour ago. Crocker's in th' pen an' Yeager's in the hospital. He's shot up bad an' they're working on him. He'll crack—maybe cracked by this time."

"He hasn't—" Carney's waning courage flared; cunning gleamed in his fishy eyes. "What d'you mean? What's all this?" His voice was loud as he could make it. "Murderer! What do you—a wanted man—mean by—!" His hand trailed across a half-open drawer.

The muzzle of Harrigan's automatic slipped over the edge of his coat-pocket. His voice was sharp with command. "Quit that, Carney! You're cinched! Drilling me and claiming self-defense won't blow up the case against you. I tell you, you're done!"

Carney stared into the yawning muzzle; his hand came away from the drawer. Harrigan was bending over him, pouring a barrage of words. Neither heeded the softly-moving girl.

"I've broken through your murder-trap, you louse! The frame wasn't strong enough to hold me! I should've come through hours ago. The sign was there but I wasn't in shape to read it. Plenty sign— You takin' all I said just to keep me here till that phone call came. Piping me down when I started to spill the dirt on Crocker so that the City-Room wouldn't hear. Squawkin' about my gun just as I opened the door!"

"Sure!" Harrigan was snarling now, his drawn face close to Carney's pale one. "But I was drunk—thanks to you an' Crocker!—and I didn't get the drift till Crocker opened up about the cane. You called him—told him I missed it. You *must've;* I didn't tell anybody else! That started it—there were other things; and now—now, do you hear?—they're breaking Yeager!"

Carney's face was pasty white. His throat worked; his hands shook; he mumbled: "No—no—I didn't—"

Harrigan's hand was on Carney's shoulder, his fingers dug into the flesh. "Man, man; don't you realize? You're an accessory to murder! An accessory before the fact—heading straight for the electric chair!"

Carney's body was a quivering mass. He jerked: "The chair—!"

Harrigan pressed the advantage, poured it in. "You've got just one chance! Call Headquarters—now!—before they break Yeager. If you beat him to the squawk, you'll beat the chair. If you stand trial, you'll fry!"

Carney seemed incapable of motion. He mouthed disjointed sentences. "It was Crocker—wanted Conwell out of the way. Wanted you away, too. You knew too much; too much about the Kane kill. Crocker was afraid. He wanted out—out of the rap and out of the racket. Got Yeager to dress like you and kill Conwell. He knew Hawkins couldn't see much—knew he was used to your clothes, your cane; figured he'd lay the kill to you. Crocker'd be in the clear—buy the *Leader;* make me Chief." His hands went limp in despairing gesture. "I knew it wouldn't work; but Crocker wouldn't let me go. He'd told me too much; he'd kill me if I didn't come in. I told—"

Harrigan said tensely: "Don't tell me, tell H.Q. You're wasting time! Losing the chance to beat the chair—"

Carney fumbled over the desk. "My ———! my ———! The chair—" Harrigan put the phone in his hand. Carney tried to hold the receiver, dropped it; mumbled thickly: "Headquarters; Police Head—"

A voice was deep at his shoulder. " 'S all right. We'll see that you get there."

Harrigan whirled in the grip of fear. A uniformed sergeant was crossing the floor. Two plain-clothesmen stood just inside the door, beyond them the little stenographer. The sergeant said: "A damn' good job, Harrigan—if we can hold him to his story."

Harrigan turned his face away said in a far-away voice: "You—heard it?"

"Yeah." The sergeant's voice was dry. "We heard him spill it, but we don't know how you got it. You'll have to come along till we check up."

The plain-clothesmen looked at Carney, grimaced at each other. They shut the door, holstered drawn guns, reached for handcuffs. The sergeant was saying: "He's all that's left if his story's right. Crocker an' Yeager shot it out. Or murder an' suicide—or somethin' queer."

Carney came alive as though pricked with needles. His hands clenched and unclenched. He said gaspingly: "Crocker— Yeager—are *dead!*"

Harrigan leaned forward swiftly, mocked with pointing finger. His voice was sneering: "Sure, they're dead! And I was like a pike on a hook! You poor fool; all you had to do was sit still. And you couldn't do it; so ——— damn' yellow you couldn't keep your clam shut!"

His hand went tight on the gun in his pocket his voice rose to heights of derision. "You're gonna stand trial alone an' fry. Get that—fry! All on account o' me—me!—the guy you thought—"

Carney half-rose in his seat. His lips drew back from gold-filled teeth. "You tricked me!" he screamed. "You lying, two-timing—" His hand streaked to the open drawer; metal shone from under papers. The sergeant stabbed at his hip. A plain-clothesman leaped forward. Madness glittered in Carney's eyes the nickel-plated gun bore down. Then Harrigan's bullet slammed him in the mouth, hurled him backward half his length—dead before he dropped.

Harrigan turned in unnatural calm; held the gun by its barrel. "All yours, Sarge. Self-defense."

The sergeant jerked away the gun, glared at Harrigan, eye to eye. "You forced his hand! Taunted him into it! Now, there's no come-back. How do we know if that confession—"

Harrigan said in a tight voice: "You heard it, didn't you? You an' the dicks an' the little girl out in the hall. It puts me over, doesn't it—right out in the clear. An' about this"—he motioned towards Carney's body—"don't squawk too loud. I did you a favor. Be a fine thing for you guys—the three of you—if a prisoner dragged a rod an' got away with a kill! Do your records good; probably get you promotions!"

He jerked away in disgust. "Come on; let's make Center Street an' clear up the details. An' for ——— sake"—his tight voice wavered and broke—"let's get a drink some place!"

Silent Heat

*Harrigan did things with a pistol
before he did things with a pen*

FRANCIS ST. XAVIER HARRIGAN came up the stairs with the purposeful air of a man who knows where he's going and wants to get there quick. His forehead was beaded with perspiration and his already dark mustache was black with it. His shirt was stuck to his spine. When he pushed back his hat, sweat streamed down his lean face. And yet outside it was cold.

At the second landing he turned to the right, heard a bell in the distance intone eleven and tapped at a darkly paneled door. There was no response. He drew down thin lips in a grimace of disgust and hit the door hard.

The wood jerked out from under his knuckles. A broad, heavy-faced man in police uniform stood in the doorway, shielding the room beyond. He growled: "Whaddaya— Oh, it's you!" Without taking his eyes from Harrigan he said over his shoulder: "Hey, Al, for ———— sake, look what's here, already!"

Al Cassidy towered into view around the edge of the door. He was tall—taller than Harrigan even—and his thin face was almost as saturnine. A bullet-cut tendon of long ago made his left leg drag a little. Over the uniformed man's shoulder, his close-lidded dark eyes looked into Harrigan's gray ones. He said in a musing, ironic tone: "Should we invite him in— maybe?"

The heavy man grunted and moved aside. Harrigan stepped through the doorway past him. His darting eyes took in the tableau.

The room was wrecked and the smell of smoke hung over it.

Bureau drawers and wads of bed ticking littered the pulled-up carpet. The upholstery had been slashed. A waste-basket full of charred papers was smoking. In the welter of the ruined bed, half obscured by the smudge from the basket, lay a woman in disarrayed black négligée. Doc Somers, a coroner's physician, was looking over what was left of her.

Harrigan's fingers tugged at his dark mustache. He said slowly: "So that's the way of it, eh?" If he felt surprise, he did not show it.

Cassidy moved around to face him, his game foot scuffing the carpet slightly. His eyes were almost closed and, far at the back of them, fires burned. He said: "Yeah, that's the way of it. An' now we'd like to know how come you're up here knockin' so soon after it happened."

Harrigan shrugged. "Any time Headquarters knows some-thin' I don't—"

"Yeah, yeah. We know you're smart. But Headquarters didn't know this till a minute ago. I just been callin' 'em up. Even if they'd let it out right away, you couldn't've possibly been here now. How come, guy?"

"Oh—that?" The reporter grinned lop-sidedly. "Just the keen Harrigan eye, Sergeant. I happened along an' saw the radio-car around the corner"—he'd seen it hadn't been in front—"an' I asked a guy which way you went. When he said up here, I gave the joint a quick up-an'-down. There seemed to be a lot o' commotion in this room—shadows passin' back an' forth on the shade—so I thought I'd drop up on the chance there was somethin' doin'." He spread slim, long-fingered hands and shrugged again. "Elementary, Watson!"

Cassidy, glancing at the window, commented: "That curtain's supposed to be shadow-proof."

"Yeah? Well, you know how those things are." He gestured towards the corpse on the bed. "Who's she?"

The Detective Sergeant's eyes turned speculatively on the reporter again.

"Don't you know?"

"Nope. Name on the bell said DeVoe. Is that supposed to mean something?"

Over in the corner, Somers straightened and cleared his throat. Cassidy turned towards him. The doctor was grinning. In one hand he held an open penknife; in the other a leaden pellet. "Stroke o' luck," he chuckled. "Drilled through the brain an' deflected downward from the skull. It was lodged just under the skin back o' the left ear." He handed the bullet to Cassidy.

The sergeant took it and strode to the center light. The burly cop crowded forward. Harrigan, moving quickly, looked over the big man's shoulder.

It was a small, sharp-nosed bullet, hardly dented at all. The cop grunted: "A .32, all right—just like we figured."

Cassidy nodded slowly. "An' silenced, probably. At least, we haven't found anyone who'll say they heard the shot."

Harrigan moved to the foot of the bed and stood looking down at the dead woman. She was somewhere over thirty; a corn-silk blonde, beginning to fade. There were puffy pouches under the eyes and hard lines at the mouth-corners. The skin was decidedly rough. With no make-up to soften the effect, the ceiling-lights were unkind to her.

Behind him, Cassidy wiped his face and slipped the slug in a vest pocket. "All right," he said brusquely, "we better get to it. The Headquarters squad'll be here soon an' we gotta see can we dig up the guy that phoned." He turned to Somers. "Sorry, Doc, your lift hadda get interrupted like this—"

Somers, clicking his bag shut, waved a hand good-naturedly. "'S all right, Cass. Don't mind that. Glad to've been along; it gave you a quicker start." He headed towards the door.

Cassidy looked at the big policeman. "You, Devens, stay here. Don't let anybody in or out till Inspector Kingdon shows. He oughta be here any minute. An' you"—he swung on Harrigan—"beat it! When Kingdon lets in the rest of the scandal-mongers, you can come too. Until then, out!"

Harrigan said in placating tones: "Aw, Cass—don't be like that now. I think y'oughta let me go with you on—"

Cassidy's thin face was dark. "Out!" he barked. "Before I change my mind. I don't like the way you breezed in here. I got half a notion t' take you down an' toss you in the hold-over. So whaddaya think now?"

Harrigan's thin lips suppressed a grin. "Ay t'ank ay go home," he said and followed the doctor out.

HARRIGAN HIT THE street three steps behind Somers and turned the other way. Half-way down the block, he spotted a lunchroom and a phone. Inside the booth, he dropped in a nickel and called a number.

A drawling feminine voice sang: *"The Morning Leader-r-r-r."*

Harrigan grunted: "Two more notes an' they'll have you out on a limb!... Nothing. Get me King—an' hurry up—"

The wire buzzed and clicked. A receiver went off at the other end and a hum of activity floated through. Then a hurried voice said: "City Desk."

"Charlie?... Listen; this's Harrigan—"

The hurried voice went staccato: "Oh. How'd you make out, Frank? D'you get it?"

"No.... Shut up, will you—an' listen!... Somebody's beat us to it. She's bumped—a .32 slug in her skull—an' the joint's been ransacked. Cassidy was there from Headquarters—an' a radio-cop named Devens. They had Doc Somers with 'em. I walked right into the middle o' things. Smack!—just like that."

City Editor Charlie King said: "——— ——— ———!" deeply.

Harrigan growled: "Yeah, I thought o' that, too—an' it didn't help a bit. She's still dead!"

He fumbled in his pocket for a cigarette; said crisply: "Listen now. I didn't crack Cassidy. I didn't say a word about the Dalton case. Headquarters doesn't know I had a check in my pocket for five grand to give to Muriel DeVoe for conviction dope on Joe Ciro. They'll find that out when they see it in the paper. We can spread that instead o' the story we didn't get!"

There was silence on the wire for a moment; then King said softly: "You mean the Ciro angle? Hell, Frank! Suppose he didn't do it?"

"Well, suppose he didn't! My ———! you don't have to *say* he did, do you?" Harrigan's tight voice rasped the disgust his lean face was registering. "Just state the facts: That we've been working up a case against Joe Ciro's white-slaving activities; that Muriel DeVoe, who used to run a place for him in Easton, agreed to tie him up with the death of Jennie Dalton, a minor; that we agreed to turn over five grand for conclusive written evidence—"

King snapped: "When I want a relief on the City Desk, I'll tell you! I got that stuff all doped out!" He chuckled a little, dryly. "But Cassidy'll sure have it in for you! By the way, we haven't had a flash on it yet. How'd Cassidy get to it?"

"Don't know for sure. It wasn't a good place to ask questions. Near's I can make it, Cassidy an' Devens were takin' Somers home in a radio-car. Somebody called Headquarters from the DeVoe apartment house an' said there'd been a disturbance or something. H.Q. sent it out on the air an' Cassidy picked it up an' went. They're just startin' the investigation now."

"Good!" The City Editor had been giving orders beside the phone. "You said the joint'd been gone over?"

"Combed! Everything in the place pulled to pieces. If Ciro didn't do it, it was somebody else that was damned anxious to beat us to anything she might have."

"Uh-huh. It musta been Ciro, all right. The fat slob! We'll

run the story as is an' head it: *Vice Czar Wanted.* Then we can call H.Q. an' tell 'em about it just before we release. By the time the sheet hits the street, the head'll be a fact!"

Harrigan said succinctly: "An' don't forget the Harrigan by-line! I'm goin' down to see the DeVoe woman's husband—"

"Okey. But that'll go for the follow-up. We'll have the kill story out by midnight!" The receiver clanged as Harrigan said: "An' don't let the rewrite guy steal the by-line."

MERVIN DEVOE LIVED in the Village, close to where Fourth Street bends into Twelfth. An actor who had been "on the verge" for years, he seemed at last to be making the grade. Astoria had okeyed him, and a ticket to Hollywood lay on his trunk. Half-packed bags were scattered about. The face that he strove to keep young was showing its age when he answered the bell for Harrigan.

The reporter was wiping his face. He grunted: "Hot, huh?"

DeVoe said in a dead tone: "You think so? Come in. You're Harrigan, aren't you? Harrigan of the *Leader?*"

The reporter raised his eyebrows. "You've heard—"

"Yes. Your paper called for a statement. They said you were coming for an interview. I have nothing to—" He sank suddenly down on the studio couch and covered his face with his hands.

Harrigan tugged at his dark mustache and squinted across at him. "Don't take it so big," he said. "After all, you haven't lived with her for—"

DeVoe spat: "Damn her!" He raised a congested face and stared at Harrigan with eyes that held hate—and despair. "Damn her! All she ever did was hurt me. She bled me as long as I had anything and when I didn't have any more, she left me. She took everything I had—every damned thing except my career—and now she's taken that!"

Harrigan had already seen the ticket. He slapped the actor on the back. "Buck up," he said. "They can't do anything to you for that. You're—"

"The hell they can't! The papers'll rake me over in connection with Muriel's murder. They'll run my pictures—stories about me. You know how Hollywood is these days. If scandal breathes on you, you're sunk!" He covered his face again. "The only thing I had left—and that she-devil's coppered me again!"

Harrigan glanced around, saw a carved oak cabinet in a corner and crossed to it. A decanter and glasses were inside. He poured a glass, drank from the side of the decanter himself, and carried the glass to DeVoe. He nudged him. "Here; take a brace for yourself."

The actor looked at it dully, took it and swallowed it at a gulp. He shuddered a little; said: "Oh, hell!" and sat up straighter on the couch. His lacklustre eyes looked at Harrigan. "From the way your City Editor spoke on the phone, I gathered you people were after Muriel before she was shot. What was it—something worse, perhaps?"

"Not for her." The reporter shook his head. "It was on the Dalton case. Y'know your wife'd been tied up with Joe Ciro—"

DeVoe's face flooded with color again. "That swine!" he choked. "That filthy, greasy panderer! If I'd been half a man, I'd have killed him when Muriel first took up with him!" His fists pounded his knees; his voice rose hysterically. "Do you hear me? I'd have killed him!"

"Yeah; he rates it, all right." Harrigan spoke soothingly, more to quiet DeVoe than anything else. "Well, Joe's been gettin' careless lately. It seems some o' these road-houses over west get a heavy play for young girls—an' Joe's been tryin' to supply the demand. You know how it works: A few shots o' hop—then a quick shut-off, an' they'll do anythin' you say. Kids that'd go straight if you left 'em alone in the first place."

The actor ground his teeth. "I know," he said.

"Yeah. Well, Joe slipped a little. He got hold of a kid dancer, Jenny Dalton—about sixteen—an' shipped her up Scranton way. The kid was pretty well gone in the hop—but not that far. She dived out of a window an' smashed her skull!"

DeVoe gasped: "The swine! The rotten, stinking louse!"

"Yeah; in spades. But they couldn't quite hang it on Joe in Pennsy. He pulled too heavy, I guess. So we started rooting it out. An' Muriel tumbled to me. She had all the dope on the Dalton girl, it seems, an' we made a deal for five grand. She wouldn't've had to appear at all. I was on my way up with the check when I found her."

DeVoe said harshly: "Ciro—?"

Harrigan shrugged. "Looks so, anyway. The place was gutted. Somebody'd been looking for something—an' the dope on the Dalton girl was supposed to be papers. Railroad stubs, an' receipts for delivery, an' nice stuff like that."

"And now—now that vulture gets in the clear?"

"Hard to tell." Harrigan glanced at the watch on his wrist. "The *Leader's* hit the street with the story already. I thought you might be able to give us somethin' on him. Every little bit helps."

DeVoe shook his head. "I wish to God I could! If I only knew—"

The reporter palmed the knob. "Read the *Leader* an' you will," he said.

He traversed the short reception hall, closed the door to the outer hall, and went slowly down the dimly lit stairs. His gray eyes were cloudy and there were vertical creases over his nose. His fingers plucked at his dark mustache. So pre-occupied was he that he had no inkling of the presence of the man whose body was flattened in the angle of the stairs.

The man, holding his breath, allowed him to pass. Then a nickeled gun chopped up and down and Harrigan, blowing out breath in a sigh, fell into waiting arms....

HARRIGAN DREAMED FITFULLY.... He dreamed he was locked in a cage and a bad man was throwing buckets of ice water in his face.... He snorted and gulped and opened his eyes. The cage was a furnished apartment; the bucket was a glass; the bad man was Joe Ciro. Harrigan mumbled: "Check!" Ciro doused him again.

Harrigan swore and struggled up. Ciro retreated hastily, his triple chin doing a jig. A hard hand caught Harrigan's coat collar and slammed him backward into a chair. A slightly nasal voice said: "An' stay there—or it gives lumps!"

Harrigan rolled his buzzing head, saw a thin young man in a pinch-back coat holding a nickeled gun, and turned back and narrowed his eyes to look at Ciro.

Joe Ciro was a frog in shirt sleeves. His dumpy body was puffed and bloated. His bald triangular head with its close-fitting ears looked less like a head than a tapering-off of his sloping shoulders. Neck he had none at all. His short legs were bowed and his feet were flat and splayed. When he spoke, it was in a succession of grunts—except when he was excited. Then he screeched.

He put down the glass, waddled around the end of a long mahogany table and plumped himself in a squeaking chair. On the back of the chair was a coat; on the table in front of him, a portable typewriter. He shoved the mill aside, reached into the coat for a blued-steel gun and fixed eyes that were almost hidden in fat on Harrigan. "Now," he grunted, "if you got somethin' to say in a hurry, I'll hear it."

Harrigan looked at the blue gun. It was a Webley; a .32-caliber automatic with a silencer clamped on the barrel. He grinned a twisted grin and said: "So that's what the DeVoe woman got it with? I should think you'd at least have wit enough to ditch the murder gun!"

Red dyed Ciro's pendulous cheeks. "Still tryin' to frame me, hey?" he yelled. "Well, when I get through with you, you'll wish you'd laid off me, you damned rat!"

Harrigan said slowly: "A rat is a useful animal, compared to a thing like you. But what makes me a rat to you, you ———?"

Ciro's whole torso quivered. He heaved himself out of the chair, rocked around the end of the table and smacked Harrigan hard with the flat of the gun. "I'll call the names!" he panted. "I'm givin' the orders here!" Saliva drooled down across his chins; his gun cracked Harrigan's head again.

Blood trickled into Harrigan's eyes. His head swung dizzily back and forth. He braced himself on the arms of the chair— tried to focus his wavering gaze on Ciro's purpled face. The gun whipped up before him; Ciro's high-pitched snarl came distantly to his ears: "An' what're ya sayin' now, huh?"

Harrigan's eyes flickered in thought; he spoke with slow concentration: "I say you're a ———!" he said. "An' ———" The flat of the gun cut it short.

The water treatment brought him around again. Ciro and the thin young man were laughing. Socking reporters around was fun, it seemed.

Ciro went to a cupboard, took out a bottle and glass and poured a drink. "Here," he grunted, "I hate to waste it like this, but I want you straightened out for a minute."

Harrigan took it and drank. It was a heavy shot and the fiery liquid coursing through him brought back some of his drained vitality. He rubbed his head, bit his tongue to keep from wincing and looked at Ciro again. "Now that we got that settled—what?"

Ciro stared at him blankly. "Now that we got what settled?"

"That you're a ———"

Ciro's jowls dropped. There was a quick step back of Harrigan's chair and the thin young man said: "Leave me sock 'im, Boss." Harrigan gripped the chair arms tensely; he was tired of being batted around. Ciro growled: "Lay off, Slim. I want 'im in shape to talk to."

The button-eyed stare came around to Harrigan. "Whatsa idea o' tryin' to frame me for the DeVoe woman's kill, huh?"

"Frame you?"

"You heard me!" Ciro leaned his gross body across the table. "You spilled out your guts about comin' to Muriel DeVoe's apartment to get her to rat on me—an' now I'm wanted for murder!" He snatched up a paper from the table and flung it across at Harrigan. "What th' hell's th' big idea?"

Harrigan caught it and spread it out. It was a midnight edition of the *Leader*. A three-column head at the right of page one said: *Ciro Wanted in DeVoe Murder. Police Believe Woman Was Shot to Insure Silence.*

And underneath:

Joe Ciro, alleged head of a huge Eastern vice ring, was wanted by police this morning in connection with the death of Muriel DeVoe, former night-club hostess, shot and killed in her apartment about ten o'clock last night.

A reporter for this paper, who arrived on the scene shortly after the tragedy, was on his way to keep an appointment with the murdered woman at which she had promised to disclose damaging evidence concerning the activities of the ring.

No arrest has as yet been made, but Ciro, alleged head of a white-slave circuit operating in New York, Massachusetts and Pennsylvania, is too well known a figure to remain in hiding long. Notorious as a racketeer, he was recently arrested in Pennsylvania in connection with the abduction of Jenny Dalton, sixteen-year-old dancer, but was freed when the girl was found dead and no witnesses against him could be discovered.

The DeVoe woman's death was caused by a .32-caliber bullet which pierced the frontal—

Harrigan's thin lips lifted the dark mustache. Eyes still on the story, he said: "It looks like you're slippin', you alleged greaseball, you!"

"Yeah?" Ciro panted the word. His face was pale and his tiny mouth was writhing across his teeth. "Yeah? You're smart, ain't you, rat? But this time, you been too damn' smart. You ain't made a statement at Headquarters yet. I found that out. An' until ya do, this stuff"—he waved at the paper—"is just a lotta horse!"

He puffed out his breath, took a gurgling swig from the

bottle and said: "Cassidy's lookin' for you now to get that state-ment. I found that out, too. An' he's plenty sore. He don't like the sudden way you showed up—an' he hates to think o' the way you snaked out on him. It all looks screwy to him. An' it won't take much to give 'im ideas."

The thin young man cackled: "Yeah—ideas."

Ciro didn't notice. He was saying viciously: "Myself, I'm wonderin' if you wasn't ridin' Muriel for a story. An' Muriel wouldn't ride—so you got tough an' somethin' went wrong. Anyway, that's the way we'll work it."

He rocked to his feet, pulled the portable typewriter close to the edge of the table and shoved a chair in front of it. Harrigan, watching him narrowly, asked: "So?"

"So we're gonna give Cassidy a leg to stand on. What he wants is a .32-caliber gun an' a motive; what I want is a lot less publicity. An' we're both gonna get what we want! Come over here!"

Harrigan's thin nostrils flared a little. "An' where do I figure in all this?"

"Oh, don't worry; you're gonna get somethin', too." The fat man picked up the Webley and nodded to the thin young man. "Bring 'im over here, Slim."

The gunman advanced grinning. Harrigan shrugged and got up.

Under the threat of the two guns, he rounded the long table and dropped into the chair. The thin young man stood across from him; Ciro, beside him, said: "There's paper in the machine. All we want is a short note, sayin' your conscience hurts you. You were tryin' to get some information from Muriel an' she wouldn't come across. You got sore an' threatened her. You didn't mean to blast her out but, some way, the gun went off. An' then you sign it."

The tip of Harrigan's tongue passed over his thinned-out lips. It wasn't bad at that—a scheme worthy of a man who fattened on crazing young girls with drugs and selling them into bondage. Backed by Harrigan's rep for getting stories in spite of hell, the thing might actually go over! He looked into Ciro's doughy face and said: "An' then I get a slug from the Webley, eh? An' the gun an' the paper are stuck in my kick an' I'm left some place I'll be easy to find!" He shook his head slowly. "No, Greaseball, I don't think I'll be havin' any o' that."

Ciro moved closer.

"You're gettin' the heat turned on you sure," he admitted. "But first, you're gonna write that note an' sign it." A wolfish leer twisted his face. "There's a dentist—a friend o' mine— downstairs. He's got the swellest collection o' burr-drills y'ever laid eyes on. We c'n rap you on the conk an' bring you down there—" He paused, ogled Harrigan's even, white teeth and said in words that slithered from him: "There's no use makin' it tough for yourself."

The reporter's jaws locked. His gray eyes were very bleak. So that was the way of it, eh? Wordlessly, he turned to the table, pulled the light machine to position and poised his fingers over the keys.

Ciro, leaning towards him, began: "To Whom It May Concern—" Harrigan's fingers, rattling the keys, paused abruptly. He bent forward, peered intently at what he had written and showed his teeth in a hard smile.

Ciro frowned heavily. "What's eatin' you now?"

"Nothin' much." The reporter spoke with savage relish. "Only this 'confession' o' mine'll probably burn you—if you make me go through with it!"

He shifted aside in the chair. "Look." His fingers grasped the typewriter, tilted it towards the fat man. "That crooked M; that cock-eyed T. Cassidy found a list o' railway-fares in the DeVoe woman's apartment. They were written on this machine. That won't tie in with me an' it'll look funny. The *Leader'll* trace it if the cops won't, an'—"

Ciro started: "What—" leaned swiftly over Harrigan. The thin man came rapidly forward, his eyes darting towards the paper. From two feet away, Harrigan smashed the typewriter into his face. His left hand flashed out, caught Ciro's right wrist and twisted the fat man in front of him.

The thin bodyguard cursed hoarsely. One hand clasped to a bleeding eye, he snapped up his gun and came staggering around the table. Harrigan, jerking Ciro around to face him, twisted the fat man's gun hand behind him and snapped: "Call off the hood—quick!"

Ciro, his forefinger strained across the trigger of the gun that was digging into his own back, screamed: "Stop! Stop, Slim! For gawd's sake—he's makin' me shoot myself!"

The thin man bared his teeth and mouthed: "The damn' louse near busted my head!" He circled to get at Harrigan.

The reporter, swinging the fat man off balance, twisted the bent wrist farther. "Call off your rat!" he grated. "You got about a second!"

Ciro's face was the color of putty; the yellow in him was washing out. "All right, Slim! All right!" He slobbered the words. "I'll see you get fixed for it, after, but lay off now—"

The hood paused, undecided. Harrigan shifted his left hand

fast, caught the Webley by the barrel—eased the imprisoned wrist. "All right," he clipped. "Let's go!"

Ciro's hand fell away. Harrigan dropped it and grasped the fat man by the collar. He jammed the muzzle of the gun over Ciro's shoulder and menaced the half-dazed torpedo. "Throw it across the room," he ordered. "Over by the door—an' don't get your directions mixed up, either."

The thin man licked his swelling lips, looked from Harrigan to Ciro, and threw the gun. It hit the lower panel of the door and banged tinnily to the floor. Harrigan, eyes flickering from one to the other, began backing slowly towards it.

When his heel struck it he bent from the knees, felt for it and picked it up. His fingers passed over it swiftly; the cartridges fell to the floor. Then, holding the empty gun by thumb and one finger, he opened the door with the rest of his hand.

Ciro gulped: "Wait! About those typewritten lists— Did Cassidy find some in Muriel's apartment that'll tie it up to me?"

Harrigan, backing out, shrugged. "You got me. He might've at that. But what the hell's the difference?" He flicked the blued-steel Webley at them. "I've got the murder-gun, now!"

He slammed the door, tossed the empty gun in the stair-well and tried to beat it down.

MERVIN DEVOE'S EYES were dull in a face from which all color had drained. His hands shook and made fumbling motions at the buttons of his pajama-coat. His legs jerked stiffly at the knees, swaying his body back and forth. He opened his mouth; said: "Gug—" thickly, and fell forward through the doorway.

Harrigan caught him around the waist, shouldered him

backward into the short reception-hall and closed the door behind him. DeVoe, unable to stand, said: "Gug-gug," unintelligibly, and rolled his eyes in their sunken sockets. The reporter picked him up and carried him bodily into the living-room.

Every light in the place was on. On a small table beside the couch, was a sheet of paper and a .32-caliber Webley with a silencer clamped on its blued-steel barrel. A fountain pen lay on the floor and, near it, an empty vial marked with the skull-and-crossbones.

Harrigan caught his breath a little, laid the semiconscious man on the couch and stooped to the paper quickly. Scrawled, sprawling script occupied part of it.

"To the police: I, Mervin DeVoe, am dead by my own hand. I thought I could go through with it but I can't. My career is finished, anyway. The publicity will—"

It trailed off there in a wavering line. The reporter sniffed at the vial, glanced again at the man on the couch and leaped to the phone in the hall.

"Hello—hello—Central! Get a doctor—quick! I know, I know—but it's life and death! Poison—I don't know what. Apartment Seven, this address!" He threw the receiver at the prong, ran back into the living-room and tore open the doors of the carved cabinet.

He slopped liquor into a glass and swung to the side of the couch. "Here, get this into you." He raised the actor's head and put the glass to his lips. "Have you got any milk—an' butter, an' stuff?"

Instead of drinking, DeVoe blew out. The liquor fountained on Harrigan's chest and a fine spray stung his eyes.

DeVoe spoke thickly: "Nuh-nuhver mind. Too late. A-an

antidote reaction'd only hurry things up." His fingers plucked at the pajama-coat again. "Fuhfeel muh heart."

Harrigan's hand slid up on the left chest. He looked startled—felt again. The faintest of faint pulse came to him.

DeVoe's smile was ghastly; his words were clearer but almost inaudible. "I'm almost gone. I started to write a confession—but I can't make it now. Letting you in overtaxed my strength." He drew in breath with a shuddering sigh. "I shot Muriel."

Harrigan's gray eyes were cloudy. He said in an absent tone: "Yeah, I figured that. A woman like her wouldn't let a man into her apartment without havin' her face made up—except maybe a husband she didn't give a damn about."

The actor's pale eyes flickered. His faint voice held fainter curiosity. "Then why—Ciro?"

"Because I hate Joe Ciro's guts! Because I'd frame a slaver any time, if I couldn't get him right! Or maybe"—The corners of Harrigan's mouth drew down; for an instant he was a leering gargoyle, mocking himself—"Or maybe, just because I'd do anything for the sake of a good story. How'd you happen to let her have it?"

"I didn't happen to." The white face worked a little. "I went there to kill her. Been there earlier in the night—pleaded with her to go to the District Attorney with the truth about Jenny Dalton. She'd laughed at me."

Harrigan's dark brows jerked. He breathed: "Jenny Dalton?"

"Yes. She was my daughter—by my first wife. Muriel always hated her. She'd been away at school—wanted to go on the stage. She came to town and I got her a spot. And Ciro"—he hissed the name—"that human wolf!—got his claws in her. She was gone before I knew it!"

Harrigan's long fingers taloned and felt the Webley under his coat. He was almost sorry he hadn't pulled trigger when he'd had Joe Ciro under the gun. He asked: "Was Muriel in on it, too?"

"I don't know. But she knew about it. She'd been drinking—and she taunted me with her knowledge. She told me I'd better get out. That a newspaper man was looking for dope on the Dalton case too. That he was coming up at eleven—and that Ciro figured he knew too much and was going to put on a party for him."

Harrigan said through shut teeth: "It was a frame-up from the beginning! She was putting me on a spot for Joe! So that's how it was they were followin' me around?"

"Yes." Harrigan had to bend close to hear it. "She wasn't afraid to tell me; thought I'd shut up on account of the papers. My career, you know. But when I heard that, I went cold; it was my chance to get back and I grabbed it.

"I had a .32-caliber Webley—the same kind of gun that I've seen Ciro carry. And I knew where I could get a silencer. I got 'em and came back. It was ten o'clock, then. I put the gun to her head and shot her."

A tremor passed over him and he paused. Harrigan's quick hand could find no heart beats and he did not seem to be breathing at all. But after a moment the pale lips fluttered and he took up the thread again.

"I figured the bullet'd hit the skull—flatten enough so it couldn't be positively identified. Then I tore up the place, burned some things in the basket and blew.

"At quarter to eleven, I called the police. I told 'em I was a tenant and that I'd heard somebody arguing in Muriel's apartment and smelled smoke coming from it. I thought they'd make it by five minutes of and probably catch Ciro right in the room.

"He'd have the gun; they couldn't be positive of the bullet. The place'd be wrecked and some papers burned. Then you'd show up and tell your story—how she was going to sell him out—"

The thin chest labored and the words were suddenly louder—gasped out on each expulsion of breath:

"I'd have done something, anyway—for the memory of my daughter—and all the other daughters—that Ciro's got—on his filthy soul!"

Harrigan said softly: "But Cassidy picked it up from a radio-car—"

"Yes. They got there—too soon. When you came here—I could see you suspected. And the policeman—"

"Policeman?"

"Yes." The pauses were very long now and the words seemed to rattle in the throat. "A sergeant—from Headquarters. Walked with a limp. He only—asked a few questions. Said he'd be back. But the reaction—was too great. Never—killed—anybody—before—"

The frail body folded together; the lined face betrayed its age; breath went out in a sighing gasp. Then, suddenly, he jerked erect; cried out in a strangling voice: "But ———— I'm not sorry!"—and fell limply back again.

The outer door was being tried; knuckles were rattling on the wood. Harrigan grunted: "About time!" and went through the reception hall to open. He didn't realize he'd been in the place only a scant four minutes.

He snapped off the catch and opened the door, saying: " 'S too late, Doc. He just—" And then a gun was deep in his belly and Joe Ciro was snarling: "Get 'em up, there—high!"

HARRIGAN GOT 'EM up. Ciro crowded him backward and kicked the door shut with his foot. They marched into the living-room.

The fat man started to close the door; rasped: "Where's—" and then the figure on the couch caught his eye. He said: "Oh—so that's it?"

His left hand passed over his bobbing chins. He grunted: "Turn aroun'—an' put your hands flat to the wall."

The reporter obeyed slowly; there was nothing else he could do. Behind him, Ciro moved to the couch and cast quick eyes over the exhibits. He grunted: "Dead, huh? I figgered the punk musta done it—an' I come over to scare it outta him!" His tiny eyes narrowed on Harrigan's bristling nape. "What'd you do with that gun you took offa me?"

The reporter hoped Ciro wouldn't frisk him. "*Leader* office, o' course," he said. "Sent it over in a cab."

"Oh, yeah?" Ciro's voice was oily. He seemed to be caressing the words. "Well, you 'n' that rag o' yours 're altogether too damn' wise. Y' been gettin' your snoot messed up in things you got no business in, an' this's a swell time to wipe it off!" He reached to the table, picked up the murder-gun and stuck his own rod in his pocket. "Turn around here, once."

Harrigan swung, saw the silenced Webley pointing at him and growled: "Well, what th' hell—"

Ciro's eyes were pinpoints of gleaming light. He jerked a finger at the corpse. "I d'no what he mightta told you, but it ain't gonna get any further, see. You're gonna stay an' keep 'im company."

The reporter shook his head. "You couldn't swing that, Joe."

"The hell I can't! It's made to order. This guy bumped his wife. You," he sneered, "bein' naturally smart, tumbled to it. You came here an' braced him. He got panicky an' let you have it with," he tapped the Webley lightly, "the murder-gun. Once you were down, he knew he was stuck. He couldn't figure a way to clear, so he took a klunk o' poison an' sat down to write it out." He leered. "Nice, huh?"

To Harrigan's ears came the faintest of clicks. He cleared his throat, thought he heard something drag lightly across the carpet, and shuffled his feet in nervous tension. He said in placating tone: "You don't mean that, do you, Joe? You wouldn't gun me in cold blood, would you?"

"The hell I wouldn't!" The fat Ciro laughed sneeringly. "It's a perfect set-up, guy. An' it gets me quit of a couple o' blokes that was gettin' bad for my business!" Without warning, his finger tightened; the gun spat flame with little noise.

But the apartment filled with roaring sound. Harrigan, diving headlong, felt a bullet whicker past his ear. Ciro screamed and fell to his knees, gripping a shattered elbow. From the little reception hall, Sergeant Cassidy shuffled in, dragging his game leg. A service gun smoked in his hand.

The reporter rolled to his knees, put close-lidded eyes on the Headquarters man and asked ironically: "You couldn't've made it a little closer, could you?"

Cassidy, holstering his gun, grunted: "I just got here. An' I saved your hide, didn't I?" His dark eyes flickered slightly. "Maybe next time you won't go holdin' out on me, huh? I been chasin' you all over hell, tryin' to find out what you *did* know about this!"

He walked close to Ciro, scooped the Webley by the barrel, and glanced at the note on the table. Vertical creases drew down his brows. He said: "Y'know I really figured DeVoe gunned her out."

Harrigan nodded. "So did I till the greaseball here busts in an' throws down on me with the murder-gun."

Ciro, moaning over his shattered arm, jerked up his bullet head. The sergeant regarded him morosely. "So we get a chance to fry you, after all, huh?"

"Me? Me!" The fat man's cheeks bobbed up and down. "————! 're you blind, flatfoot! This ————'s tryin' ta frame me again! DeVoe done it an' bumped himself off. There's the note on the table. Can'tcha read!"

Harrigan laughed harshly. "He's a quick thinker, Sarge. Just because poor DeVoe couldn't take it, saw the publicity bustin' up his career an' passed himself out, the greaseball wants to make a confession of it an' stick him for the kill!"

Ciro screamed: "No! No! For ———— sake! He's framin' me!"

Cassidy looked from one to the other.

Harrigan said quickly: "The note says nothin' about a killing. It was just that DeVoe couldn't take it. An' hell! who had the murder-gun, fixin' to leave it here, alongside my dead body? You heard it, yourself, when—"

"Yeah, yeah." The Headquarters man was sarcastic. "Go on now, draw the diagram!" He jerked his head at Ciro. "C'mon, louse, get up an' take your first steps on the road to the chair!"

Ciro's eyes were wild. They swiveled from Harrigan to Cassidy, and back to the mocking reporter again. He shrieked a curse, whirled to his knees and dug at his left-hand pocket.

Cassidy yelled: "Look out!" and leaped. Harrigan's hand flashed under his coat. One gun roared and another whispered—and Joe Ciro pitched on his flabby face, a neat blue hole just under his lowest chin.

The reporter looked at his punctured hat and held out a gun to Cassidy: a .32-caliber Webley with a silencer clamped on the barrel. "Here," he said; "it's some more o' the greaseball's arsenal. I forgot to turn it over to you. There'll be some o' his prints alongside o' mine."

Cassidy's saturnine face was wooden. "There better be," he said.

Harrigan grinned lop-sidedly. "There will. I took it away from him, while ago. An' the bullet that was in the DeVoe woman comes from the other one, anyway." His fingers passed under his collar. "Damn, it's hot!"

About the Author

ED LYBECK WAS born in England, reared in Sweden and is now a voter in the good old U.S.A. Has been an office boy, waiter, professional dancer and a semi-pro ballplayer, and as far as he is personally concerned, is an all-around work-hater. Has contributed to periodicals, magazines and other newspapers, but his first choice is to write true stories.